DOUBLE HOLME
John Pirillo

CW01466953

Copyright 2023, John Pirillo

"A Date with Death," previously published as "Mesmer's Eyes."

A DATE WITH DEATH

Holmes

The least amount of effort can provide the maximum amount of profitable knowledge under certain circumstances; but the maximum deduction of facts and clues will always lead to the proper conclusion.

—Sherlock Holmes

Doctor Franz Anton Mesmer

Vienna, Austria

Madam Bouvet and her circle of friends were absolutely amazed by the tricks that Doctor Franz Anton Mesmer, a physician gaining more and more notoriety of late...even matching that of the mad Russian Rasputin, who was reported to have similar abilities.

But he gave it no second thought.

"It's the eyes that have it," he explained to his enthralled audience. "And the voice."

Madam Bouvet smiled at him. "Dear Doctor, you are such an exciting man. Whatever in the world made you come up with this mad practice of yours...this...this..."

"Mesmerism?"

"Yes, that ism."

Everyone laughed.

He gave her a patient nod. She and the ones invited were important to his research, so he did not mock or scold them like he might have listening children, even though they were like children the way they held themselves enthralled by his simple science of the mind.

"Mesmerism will one day become the standard medical practice of the world," he went on. "The masses will be cured by its influence."

"Surely not all?" A short midget, barely visible in the back of several other people, asked.

Doctor Mesmer turned towards the direction of the voice and frowned. He couldn't see the person speaking; but he certainly knew the scoffing tone of it.

"I never said everyone. Only that the masses would be cured. Those who had no possibility of a cure, soon will."

Doctor Mesmer's right eye twitched nervously as he stared at his audience, surveying for the results of his explanation, determining if his influence had just been undermined or not.

"But how can your science cure anyone?" That voice asked again.

He bristled with anger at the repugnance of the statement, but said nothing. Do not throw pearls before swine came to his mind and he bit his words back, though he felt a taste of bile rising into his mouth from his disgust at this horrible man's words.

"Because I have used it to cure over one hundred patients."

Exclamations of wonder from the audience, except for the hidden man, who had other things on his mind now.

Doctor Mesmer stood at t he front of the small auditorium sized living room that was adorned with black and red drapes for the occasion, hiding the very expensive paintings of Gaugin, Ecker, Galileo and Destry...all noted for their mystical backgrounds and somewhat dark interpretations of fantasy and magic.

Galileo did have touches of Light in his, but the church always figured ominously somehow in the symbol he used, knives, pikes, swords, and spears and always with blood stains on them.

Stains the man felt from the abuse the church had heaped upon him for his discoveries before in disgust he had finally given up trying to convince the world of it not being the center of the multiverse and retreated into the lonely life of an abstract artists.

While Galileo's and the other artists were not individually associated with the dark arts, their artwork surely summoned up imagery that made one shudder at first glance and then quickly retreat from them to preserve one's equanimity, if not sanity. Dark magic maybe not, but dark impressions...most certainly!

In abundance.

Also stationed about the large living space, which usually on the weekend, which this was, there would be tables set with condiments, salads, sweets and sliced hams, and beef for the guests, a small five man orchestral team playing softly in the background, a poet such as Byron, Smirtz, Pirillo, or Poe auditioning to the glee and sometimes amusement of their listeners, their latest stabs at dark humor and sometimes Divine statements being heard and often times discoursed by the would be intellectuals of the audience, who hadn't a clue what intellectual even meant, let alone how to use their higher faculties for anything other than spending their wealth.

Byron was known to be quite the flirt with the men and Poe with the ladies. As for Smirtz and Pirillo, both men seemed somewhat withdrawn and polite, but remote from any kind of sexual contact at all...even to the shaking of hands...for which they wore gloves.. Pirillo, white. Smirtz, black.

Symbolic of higher and lower aspirations. One never knew. But definitely symbolic of something, even if not directly understood.

"Doctor Mesmer," a man's voice called from the back of the large room.

Doctor Mesmer shook out of his unresponsive reverie upon the second call for attention.

"Doctor Mesmer!"

He jerked around. It was the smaller man again. If smaller could be adequately supplied to such a creature as now faced him.

But a man of politeness he was, even though it galled him to favor this monster before him with a dignity that the creature most certainly did not deserve.

"Sir?" He asked, forcing a thin smile to his lips.

A midget standing little over two feet tall climbed onto a chair to be seen and waved his arm.

Everyone turned to look and then parted somewhat so the doctor could see him clearly.

He would have gasped. He knew much about human character and much about what a person's true nature was by the sound of their voice; but to have his darker observations so thoroughly affirmed, at this moment frightened him.

"Is it true you've caused a goat to mate with a duck using your mesmerism?"

Stunned silence.

Then titters, then louder laughter.

The midget smiled, but his smile might as well have been an explosion of poisoned darts smashing into Doctor Mesmer's body for how badly he felt at that moment.

The midget continued. "I think, if true, that would be quite hilarious. I imagine the poor duck would have a dark night of it afterwards."

Shocked cries of alarm. Now he had gone too far. A joke...even a titillating one of gentle nature can be tolerated, but this was beyond a joke and reaching into the realms of deeply humiliating and insulting.

Doctor Mesmer eyed the midget. "You are coarse, sir."

Madam Bouvet stepped from the crowd where she had been standing to confront the midget. His smile was not lost, nor his stance on the c hair. If anything, he seemed more aloof and antagonistic than before by the way he crossed his arms, puffed his fat chest out and squeezed his jaws by tightening his jaws, like a bulldog with a grip on its pray.

The disgusting man wore a top hat that looked straight from a circus. His girth did not match his wit; for it was well rounded. Surely the midget weighed as much or greater than a man of some height.

"I do not know your name. I invited you here?" She queried him in a cold, solemn voice.

Doctor Mesmer felt some relief. Madame Bouvey could be quite tough when need be. He crossed his arms, waiting for the usual submission and apology she would extract from the weak and vulgar.

The midget took his hat off and made a bow. "No, you did not, I'm proud to say."

More cries of alarm.

Madam Bouvet's eyes narrowed. Her breath caught in her throat and hands clenched into fists.

Good, she shall show him who's the one in charge her, Doctor Mesmer thought cheerfully, eager to see it happen.

Some of the men about the midget turned hard of face and moved towards the man, preparing to throw the blaggart out on his head if he didn't change his tone.

Madame Bouvet motioned for them to stop.

They did, but did not lose their looks of anger , or stares as hard as cold steel upon the midget.

"Your name?" She asked, pretending not to have heard his insults or dismissal of her in his rude and vulgar reply. No one comes to her parties uninvited. Not without a cost upon their heads!

He gave her a second bow, revealing this time as she looked more closely that he had some kind of pattern tattooed on the top of his shiny bald scalp.

He straightened. "I received my mark in the Chinas."

He looked her directly in the eyes, a sneer on his lips. "You were looking at the mark and not the rest of my pleasant body, I'm sure."

She gasped, then immediately reached for the fire poker by the fireplace where she stood. Before she could grasp it, Doctor Mesmer took a step back and put a hand on her arm. "I am not insulted by his question good Madam

Bouvet. Nor should you be. I suggest you forgive his rude behavior and we proceed as if he were invited."

The midget smiled. "I agree!" But the dangerous look that had grown in his eyes when he saw her reach for the fireplace poker didn't diminish or vanish. If anything, his eyes seemed to have come to life in some kind of mysterious way.

Again a man turned to rush the midget. But when he attempted to move towards the midget, his feet became like barrels of heavy stone. He couldn't move them even a tiny bit.

"Sir, what is your interest in that black mark upon your skull. To what end do you reveal this to us now?"

"I am a fellow practitioner of your craft, Doctor. Except it is not called Mesmerism as your colleagues and building audience of followers use for you."

He touched his scalp as if petting something alive. "No, what I learned in the Chinas far exceeds your crude Mesmerism as it's called."

"Then what is it?"

"Mysterius."

"There is nothing mysterious about mesmerism. It's a proven science."

"I agree."

"Then what is your disagreement with me."

"Oh, not with you, but the buffoons who glorify you when they should be giving my craft the greater attention."

For the first time that night Doctor Mesmer felt truly and deeply offended, to the extent that he was no longer filled with any regret for the next words that would come forth from his mouth. He beat the midge with them.

"You are crass and a coward to lass out at our kind hostess and me, when all you have to your name is empty words. One more word and I shall challenge you to a duel!"

"Go ahead. It won't do you any good."

"You challenge the great Doctor Mesmer?" Madam Bouvet asked in astonishment, ready to trounce the short fellow herself.

"He challenges a genius; I merely challenge a fool whose knowledge is superficial and will change nothing of the world, except for the pocketbooks of those who practice his crude science."

Now Madam Bouvet couldn't hold the men back even if she threw her body in front of them.

They all tried to rush at the same time.

And at the same time all found themselves incapable of moving a single muscle.

"What have you done to us?" Demanded a husky German, whose shoulders were so broad you could have stood a grown man on either side and still not caused a dimple in the man's height.

"ENOUGH!" Doctor Mesmer shouted in his loudest voice. He plucked a wand from his suit and waved it at the midget. "You name sir before you die?"

He might not be able to affect the man with Mesmerism, but magic never failed. He pressed the wand outwards, energies gathering at its tip.

"Oh, I shan't die, Doctor by your crude weapon."

"You will relent or I shall punish you severely," Doctor Mesmer cried out. "You have stepped too far. But I am a forgiving man, apologize and leave and you may het live!"

The midget coughed into a hand, then chuckled, not in the least alarmed.

"Tomorrow at sun's rise; here in Madame Bouvet's yard you shall die, sir," Doctor Mesmer shouted at the midget. "I cannot forgive this further. Upon my honor your foul presence shall be erased from this planet and sent to the hell it obviously originated from."

Doctor Mesmer caught himself and glanced at Madame Bouvet. "With your permission of course?"

"Of course." She turned to look at the midget. "Your name sir. I wish to extend invitations to your slaughter so you will be long remembered."

The midget grinned. "My friends call me Mysterio."

"What do your enemies call you?"

"I do not have any enemies."

"Impossible!"

"Not at all," the midget replied. He made a gesture and then a man cried out in alarm and clutched at his throat and gagging began to turn blue in the face.

Then another.

Another.

And another.

Each falling as the midget gestured at them.

Finally, he looked at Madame Bouvey. "Do you understand me now?"

He smiled as she began to make gagging sounds.

She clasped her hands to her throat, trying to open up her breathing. But to no use. She began to falter on her legs.

Doctor Mesmer caught her and turned an angry eye on the midget. "Sir, I shall have you now!"

"I doubt it! Even your Mesmerism will not be enough to save you now."

Doctor Mesmer let go of Madam Bouvet and clutched at his own throat, gasping for air the same time as she fell lifeless to the floor.

He glanced at Mysterio with great fear in his eyes.

"Ha…. ha…how?"

He collapsed to the floor joining the others of the party who were now laying lifeless on the floor.

Mysterio dropped from the chair and walked daintily over to look at the man who was beginning to lose consciousness. "Wouldn't you like to know?"

"Wh…wha…. why?" Doctor Mesmer choked out, collapsing to his knees, clutching at his throat.

"You'll never know."

"Yo…you….your…."

Doctor Mesmer fell onto his side. He managed to look up as Mysterio dropped to a knee to look into his face.

"How?"

Mysterio chuckled. "What you failed to learn with your stupid science is that the eyes are the windows not only to the soul, but to the power of a god."

He smiled, his face turning dark and vicious now.

"Yes.. The eyes have it, pardon the rather unlovely joke."

He leaned closer to whisper in Doctor Mesmer's right ear. "You only guessed one part of what Mesmerism is; I learned all of it."

Mysterio rose suddenly and then gave the great doctor a powerful kick in the skull, sending him expediently and more quickly into the next life.

Mysterio chuckled, glanced at all the fallen men and women scattered about the small auditorium, in poses of surprise, shock and horror. Faces purple and blue

from suffocation.

He bowed to them all. "I introduce to you *The Great Mysterio, Our World's Greatest Mesmerist*!"

Then he smiled warmly. "Yes, the eyes have it. All of it."

And person by person he moved about the room, gathering the fuel for his power.

Sherlock and Juliet

"Juliet," she told him.

Holmes eyed her uncertainly. An uncomfortable name for him, having just seen Shakespeare's play the other night and mourning the loss of the tragic and doomed romantic couple.

Life was not pleasant for the young in those times. Nor was it so much more now with the massive poverty that enshrouded modern London, despite all its technological wonders.

Which was accented in his mind as one of the huge Naval Warship flew noisily past overhead, its huge tripellers swirling about on the extensions below its tri hull, pushed by massive steam engines that converted steam into electricity to power its massive cannon and battlements.

She saw his frown and where he was looking. "Why do men war upon men?"

"Because they are children."

She smiled. "You are not?"

"I am at times."

She laughed. "Humility. I like that."

He smiled back. "How is it that I have never seen you before?"

"Because you never looked."

Holmes gave her a questioning look.

"Mother asked that if I do visit London, I do so incognito. You are the first and last to have recognized me for what I am."

"And what is that, may I ask?"

"A woman who will not break your heart."

He laughed, then realized she was serious.

"I think you would be a challenge in a game of chess."

She dimpled. "Oh, I am just terrible at chess. I only win three out of four times."

His spirits picked up. "I would enjoy playing with you."

She gave him a coy look. "I suspect I would give you much joy doing that as well."

Holmes offered his arm. "I'd like to take you to a very special place...if I may?"

"You're not afraid of being snubbed for my looks?"

Holmes shook his head. "I don't judge a man or woman by their looks, but by their actions. Words can be deceiving, thoughts can be hidden, but one's actions can never be lost to the observant eye."

"Well, in that case," she said with a smile creasing her face warmly, causing her eyes to glow as well. "I accept."

She slid her hand over his arm and he strolled from the alley with her by his side.

And as they talked on the way to the special place he had planned to take her, neither of them saw or heard another living soul, car, plane or animal...because both saw nothing else but each other.

Mysterio

William Shakespeare accepted the usual applause front stage, bowing slightly to acknowledge the love of his theater audience, then gestured to his right where a man, quite large and heavy, was on the stage canvas, head between his legs and hands before him as if bowing.

"Let's give a hand to the volunteer."

Laughter.

Peals of laughter.

Cheers.

Clapping.

Shakespeare, or Willie as most liked to call him flipped his pony tail over his other shoulder, then gave a gesture to a man hiding on purpose in deep shadows to his right.

"Let's also give a hand to the world's greatest Mesmerist, Mysterio, who shall perform a miracle tonight on stage in front of your very eyes with the man to my right."

Shakespeare steps aside and Mysterio moves in the deep shadow, only his eyes showing. And they are powerful...and frightening as he gazes at the volunteer, who sees the eyes for the first time.

"Sir, you will now stand on your pinkie!"

The crowd broke into laughter.

"Impossible!" Yelled a man, elbowing his wife as he watched.

"You're a dratted idiot to think a man that size could stand on his pinkie," insulted a second man, who also gave his wife a snicker.

Both men were going to regret those words later. But for now the audience loved them. No one could see the expression of pure hatred on Mysterio's face after their words.

Had they, they might have fled for their lives. But they did not. The continued to rail at him.

Big mistake.

The men, thinking they had won over the audience with their taunting of the Mysterio, rose from their seats and took quick bows and then their wives to the amusement of the females in the audience.

They couldn't see the expression on Mysterio's face or they might have immediately sat back down and even apologized for their rude manners. But they didn't and would pay for their mistakes.

More applause, then an expectant silence as the man on Shakespeare's right grunts, "I'm getting dizzy."

The crowd had forgot about the big man during their taunting and teasing of Mysterio, but now they can plainly see a miracle before their eyes. The crowd jumps to their feet and roars with approval as the big man manages to elevate himself upside down on his pinkie finger before the amused and amazed eyes of the crowd.

Amazed, because not a one there believed it humanly possible to support that much weight upon such a small finger.

Amused, because the poor chap's pants fit too loose and are now bagging down , revealing thick heavily haired legs with large freckles on the ankles.

"You may come down now."

The man drops to his knees and blinks.

He eyes his pinkie.

"Does it hurt?" Mysterio asks as he steps forth from the deep shadows.

The big man looks up at the man who is asking.

A rotund man who is almost as wide as he is tall and who wears a top hat that is almost as tall as he stands. Mysterio.

Mysterio's face sprouts a thick mustache that curls at the tips into barbed points. His eyes are a menacing deep black when not smiling, but at the moment, a smile lights his face, though not the kind one would want across from oneself at a dining table.

"Not at all."

The big man lowers himself to the stage and looks at his pinkie as if it were something strange on his hand, instead of his own finger. "I stood upside down on my pinkie?"

"You did."

Mysterio turns to the large crowd seated in the auditorium of the Globe Theater, where Willie...William Shakespeare...stands at the front row of the audience, a smile on his face.

Willie likes to see what is going on as if he were part of the audience and usually sits in the front row, or sometimes in the balconies, so he can see what the audience is experiencing.

Willie has sold out for two weeks in a row now and the concessions will make him enough money to live for a year without another crowd pleaser, which sometimes his own productions are not.

Shakespeare turns to the audience. "He did. You saw it with your very own eyes, didn't you?"

The crowd bursts into applause and cheers.

Then the big man realizes something else that is surprising to him. His pants are no longer bagged over his waist, but fallen down to his ankles. He did this himself as the crowd watched in amazement.

Mysterio grinned, knowing he had given the command as the big man was falling to his knees to get back to his feet.

The big man let out a yowl of surprise and embarrassment, grabbed his pants back up and hightailed it for the curtain, ripped it aside and tore backstage to find the nearest exit. All to the laughter of an amused audience.

A pleased audience.

Shakespeare heard the ting ting of silver and gold coin falling into his treasure box this night at the sound of applause.

When the applause dimmed, Mysterio smiled at the audience and gestured to a side curtain which opened to reveal dozens of red roses laying in a heap there.

"Who would like a rose?"

Hands jumped into the sky.

Mysterio waddled to the apron edge of the stage and looked down.

He checked the audience over, as if searching for just the right ones to give a rose too.

The audience leaned forward in expectation.

Shakespeare rubbed his palms together in glee. He knew this would sell more confections for him and guarantee that more would attend the later performance as well. Even some of the same ones staying for the next performance.

"Ah," Mysterio said in a deep, but kind of gravelly voice. "You and you..."

He gestured to the first couple that had insulted him.

"And you two as well," he added, pointing to the other couple who had insulted him.

Both couples rushed to the front stage to accept their roses, faces lit by happy smiles. This was going to be the best day of their lives. They could feel it. Luck was on their side.

Both couples had forgotten that earlier they had insulted this short man, humiliated him in front of hundreds.

But he hadn't forgotten.

As the accepted their roses, one by one, he gave them each a smile.

A smile that none noticed because of their prizes claiming their attention more.

Had they noticed, perhaps their nights would have turned out differently. Perhaps.

31 Gable Street

Harry ruffled the hair of young Manley. "I love the way you bring the paper to us every day, Manley."

"Well, my pleasure, sir."

Harry eyed the blonde haired kid with the startling blue eyes. "Never know when a good deed will pay off."

"No sir. Never."

A ritual that Harry goes through every time Manley comes to collect for his paper route.

"Well then, how much do we owe you, lad?"

"Ten pence."

Harry frowns.

Manley gives him a worried look.

Harry grins, then gives Manley ten pounds. "Will that cover it?"

"Sir! That's too much!"

Harry grins. "Big surprises come in such small moments some times."

He shut the door and leaned against it to listen.

He was reward with the sound of Manley screaming happily, his feet stomping down the stairs to the exit from the building.

"You're such a spoiler, dear?"

Harry turned to give his wife a good, long hug. "Some spoils are best given in large measures."

"Well, in that case, maybe I should give you one."

She took his hand and started guiding him towards the bedroom, but instead of ending up there, they ended up at the cabinet where Harry kept his pistols. He had acquired them as part of a growing collection. He had loved guns since a child.

"Now why are we here?" He asked.

"I don't know," she replied, giving him a surprised look.

But she didn't stop with the look. No, instead, she reached into the cabinet and took one pistol out and handed it to him and another for herself.

Still holding hands, they went to the center of their sitting room, both smiling. She aimed her weapon at his heart and he did the same with her.

"Well now..."

"Indeed," she replied. "Well now, indeed."

"I suppose it's about that time anyway," he said with a grin.

"I love it when you grin, Harry."

"Me too. It makes me feel warm and fuzzy all over."

Harry smiled as his trigger finger tightened. His pistol did not waver. His glance did not either.

"Very nice of the man to give us so many roses."

His wife grinned at him, "Extremely. We should have thanked him for them."

"But we can't."

"No," she agreed warmly. "We can't."

"I love you so much," he told her.

She smiled. Nodded. "I still remember the first night we met at the garden party."

"You were all pretty in pink chiffon."

"And you in that handsome suit and tie."

"My tie had tea stains."

She laughed. "But I loved you anyhow. From the very first moment our eyes met."

"And I."

"Our neighbors won't like this."

"Who cares what they think? We didn't care when we ran off against their best wishes to get married, now, did we?"

"True. And I've never regretted that."

"Or I."

"You don't think he's going to make us do this, do you?"

"The fat midget we insulted."

"Mysterio. Yes, him. He had such a lovely smile when he told us what to do when he came to visit us."

"Yes, he did."

"But I don't remember him knocking on the door to let him in."

"He don't need doors evidently."

He burst into laughter.

She joined him.

They lapsed into silence, still frozen in a posture of weapons poised to fire.

"I don't want to end this."

"I don't either, but he said we had to do this."

"Why?"

"You know why, Harry. We was bad to him. And he can't let us go unpunished. We'd be like little kids getting off the hook for being naughty."

"True."

She smiled. "Love conquers all!"

He sighed. "Not everything. We still have pressing bills." Then he nodded to his gun. "And now this as well."

"Yes. This too," She agreed, nodding to her own weapon.

"Look on the bright side of it, my dear."

"I don't see one."

"We won't remember."

She laughed. "Well, that most certainly puts a stopper to everything, doesn't it now?. She felt a tear loosening in her right eye. "I'm sorry."

"I love you."

"I love you too. But we can't be naughty."I'm sorry, we can't disappoint the good man."

"I agree. We were not very nice to him," she whimpered, sniffling, beginning to shake.

He handed her a handkerchief from his suit pocket.

She took it and blew in it with one hand.

"We made a mistake."

"Yes, we did."

"And now we're going to pay for it."

"Yes. We are."

"Why?"

"Because we opened our mouths at the wrong time..."

"...To the wrong person."

"He's such a hateful man."

"He is."

They both turned as the grandfather clock began to chime the hour.

"Soon now, darling."

She smiled. "Too soon."

"I remember the smile on Shakespeare's face at the end of the performance.

"

"As do I."

"We shouldn't have jeered the small man."

"Mysterio? No. We probably should have not."

"That was a mistake."

"A big mistake."

He looked again at his weapon. "I can't put it down. Can you?"

Her body began to shake, her hand quiver, but the pistol hand remained fixed on him. She began to weep. "Not an inch."

"Love shouldn't die like this."

"It won't die. We're like Shakespeare's Romeo and Juliet."

"They both died."

"Yes, they did."

"We're going to die, aren't we?"

"Not if I can help it."

"But you can't."

His body began to shake and quiver now. Sweat formed on his brows. "No, I can't."

His weapon also didn't budge an inch.

"I'd hug you but I'm afraid this will end sooner."

"I think you're right," she said, taking a step closer to him.

Her trigger finger tightened.

When she stepped back it didn't tighten further, but it didn't loosen either.

"I'm sorry," she sobbed.

"Don't be," he told her, his eyes warm with love and affection. "These have been the best two months of my life."

"Better to have loved and lost..."

"...Than never to have loved at all," she finished for him.

They both broke into laughter.

A family of pigeons that roosted on their windowsill looked inside, startled, then took to the air at the sound of two pistol shots.

Pier One

Thames.

The sun was just setting.

Its glorious radiance was a day long ending to a lifelong event for two lovers. Not of body, but of soul. They sat side by side on the edge of the pier, both with shoes off and beside them.

Hers ragged and with holes in their toes.

His highly polished and clean as the mirror surface of just swiped glass.

She leaned against him.

"I feel as if we've known each other forever."

He smiled.

"When I was in India, I always wondered what true love would feel like."

"And?"

He turned to look into her eyes. "I am still wondering, but perhaps a bit less."

She laughed, her eyes sparkling and dancing with the reflected light of the setting sun.

"Tell me why you went there?"

"Father felt I should be more worldly. Not close minded like so many who have never traveled. He wanted me to see just how large our universe was."

"I hardly think a trip to India qualifies as seeing the entire universe."

He chuckled. "I love the way you laugh."

"I love laughing. I hate being serious all the time like mother is."

He nodded. "She sounds like a wise person."

"Do all wise people not laugh?"

"No. But they when not to."

She laughed again and leaned more into hm.

Holmes felt this sudden impulse to kiss her, but shoved it down deep. He didn't know how to deal with these new feelings.

He had betrayed himself once with Destiny. Twice he had given his love to her and twice she had broken his heart.

But something about this woman next to him told him it wasn't a lie. That she did indeed care for him.

But how was that possible in such a short period of time?

Pahalgam, India

Holmes and the Monk, his teacher and friend and master, walked at a good pace along the banks of the Ganges. The hanging bridge was about two miles behind them now and quickly becoming invisible in the descending darkness of night falling.

They passed a young man who was laying flowers at the grave of a someone long gone. He could tell that because the marker for the loved one was old and worn. Years had passed. Perhaps dozens. Perhaps decades and decades.

They passed the young man, who was singing happily to himself.

"Why is he singing if he is mourning a lost one?"

The Monk didn't slow down, but kept going. "Because the past is gone and now the future is about to dance forth in all its glory."

"Like the sun when it's morning?"

The Monk stopped. "Time is an illusion, Sherlock. It's marked by sun and moon, but only so man can have some sense of balance in his life. For a man who has no attachments in his life, there is not time, no night, no day. It's all just now."

"Sounds like of boring."

The Monk laughed. "That's because I'm describing a state of being and not a state of presence. To the man experiencing the timelessness, he is still treading between light and dark and late and early, but his motives, his drive, his awareness is centered and therefore not affected negatively by either. His life is one with the purpose of all that is."

"That also sounds boring."

The Monk sat down on a large boulder that overlooked the roaring Ganges to their left.

Holmes joined him.

"Look at it this way, Sherlock."

"How?"

"Men, philosophers, wise and not so wise. They spend so much of their life trying to figure out life, to put a harness on it, rather than just allowing it to direct them to the proper destinations."

He gestured to the Ganges.

"If a man becomes like the waters of the Ganges, then he will flow along and through the channels of life, moving first this direction, more of another, but always flowing endlessly forward."

"But man is not water."

"Sherlock, man can be like water. He need only let go of his needs to control everything in his life and listen to the still voice within."

"Isn't that what the Christians teach? And you are Hindu."

"No, Sherlock, I am merely a man."

"And do you flow along the banks of life, letting yourself be guided to where ever it wishes to take you?"

The Monk looked at Holmes for a long time, saying nothing, then said, "The true question, dear Sherlock, is do you?"

Rooftops

A family of pigeons were pecking peacefully on the roof of 31 Gable Street when a sharp sound snapped their heads around and then a second sent them hurtling into the sky, crying out in alarm.

Neighbors flushed their windows open and peered out in alarm.

A constable on the beat stopped twirling his nightstick and glanced sharply to his right.

Gun shot?

No! Two!

An old model steam-powered car, which still used gas as well, let out a huge popping sound that cracked like a whip.

The constable relaxed, and began twirling his nightstick again.

"Dratted rattletraps," he cursed. "Someone should get those old buggies off the road. They can give a poor sod a heart attack, they can."

But then he gave it no more thought and continued his beat, turning off Gable Street onto Oliver and passing from view, his only thoughts about the cute young bar maid he met the last night and was seeing again tonight for other matters more pleasing to the mind.

221B Baker Street

Holmes attention snapped to the right at the sound of a sharp retort in the near distance.

His eyebrows furrowed.

Watson peered out the windows from above.

"Hear that, Holmes?"

"I did."

"Good, I'll be right down."

Holmes sighed and shoved his package he had been carrying under his left arm beneath his right.

Several long moments later Doctor John Watson stuck his mutton chopped face out the front door after he opened it, the peered out cautiously, as if expecting someone to assault him.

Holmes shook his head. "Watson, really!"

"Can never be too careful you know."

Then Watson saw the package. "For me?"

"Not unless you wear a dress."

"For Mrs. Hudson?"

"I would not dare to presume such a thing."

"Then for whom?"

Watson adjusted his jacket and hat, then came down the stairs, a black bag in his right hand. He never went anywhere without it. It carried important medical equipment, and more importantly maps. He was always losing his way when he traveled with Holmes, who had the sense of direction of a bloodhound.

"Then for whom?" He repeated as he reached Holmes.

"A gift."

"For whom?"

Holmes finally smiled. "John, you are too predictably stubborn when it comes to giving up on a course of action."

"Which is precisely why you have chosen me as your investigative partner."

"I thought it was because you slept without snoring."

"Why would you hear me doing that?"

"Because you always forget to close your bedroom door and if you did snore, knowing how sensitive my hearing is, I would be awoken immediately by it."

"It's not as if snoring were a horrible or deadly thing."

"Then you never heard my grandfather."

Watson laughed.

Holmes snickered. "And I pray you never have to."

"You never talk much about him."

"Not much to talk about. He's quite reclusive. Stays inside day and night reading the latest medical journals, coming up with theories and practical methods of investigative methods."

"Which you, undoubtedly, scrape his brains for."

"Indeed."

"So what is it?"

"A dress."

"But you still haven't said for whom?"

Gillum Way and Remorse

Watson stopped a moment on their walk to admire a poster on the wall beside a cake store. "I wonder if the show is doing any good?"

Holmes peered at the poster. It showed a rotund man with an elephant balancing in the palm of his right hand. "I would imagine if he can balance an elephant in the palm of his right hand he would have an endless stream of admirers."

"Willie is quoted here as saying this man is the greatest mesmerist of our time."

"Really? I thought that Doctor Mesmer owned that title."

"He's a dead man, Holmes."

"Ahh, so you do read my journal sometimes?"

Watson blushed. "Well, you leave the bloody thing on the sitting room table wide open beside the tray of scones. What do you expect?"

"No less, dear John. No less. And you're welcome to any of the facts I do record within it."

"But it's true though."

"What is?"

"That Shakespeare calls this man the greatest mesmerist ever."

Holmes smiled. "Willie says that about all his acts."

He and Watson continued on.

Watson chuckled. "I imagine Willie would. He is known to have a rather large sense of humor as well as a touch of gigantism when it comes to telling a tale or two."

Holmes glanced at his partner and gave him a grin. "As one good doctor walking beside me tends to do when recording our adventures together. We don't destroy vampires and werewolves every night and day as you sometimes claim."

Watson chuckled. "No, but it does keep the audience interested and staying with my stories until they're finished when I do say those things."

Holmes clapped a hand on Watson's shoulder. "If you did anything less, I'd be disappointed and have to ask where my good friend had vanished to."

"Mrs. Hudson's cupboard to steal some fresh scones!"

They both laughed a long time, then feeling warm and comfortable with each other, they both wiped at tears in their eyes, doing t heir best to hide it. Both men loved each other dearly, but rarely displayed such affection in words for fear of coarsening the depth and breadth of their affection for each other.

Holmes and he lapsed into an amiable silence, breathing in the fresh air, feeling the blood rush to their heads from the brisk walk. And most certainly from that refreshing and warm burst of humor and laughter.

Suddenly, Holmes caught Watson by his arm as he was about to pass an alleyway they began to cross.

"Here we stop, Watson."

"Very well." Watson stared at the alley which intersected Gillum Way and Remorse. "But why an alley? Surely no one lives therein?"

Holmes gave him a sad look. "I wish it were so. Come."

Holmes strode into the alley, his cape flowing a bit behind him as the draft which came through the alley struck it and lifted it behind him, giving him a gay look, like a racing car driver of the new electric vehicles that were the wonder of this world.

Watson's eyes blinked repeatedly as they tried to adjust to the darkness therein the alley and also to discern what appeared to be of all unlikely places, a crude shelter of some kind.

Holmes didn't slow down.

Finally, he reached the shelter and stopped.

Watson was about to say something, but Holmes waved a hand for quiet.

Watson waited, though God knew for what.

As if the heavens had opened a female voice began singing from within the crude shelter, starting low and husky and then as if refining itself in the process of the song drove upwards into a beautiful series of melodic high notes that trilled like a canary's might, gathering strength and robustness.

Watson stood there, mesmerized by the quality, depth and emotion of the voice.

Holmes stood next to him, eyes shut, a smile on his face as if he had entered the doorway to heaven.

Finally, the singing stopped.

Silence.

Watson opened his eyes.

"What!" He was surprised he had shut his eyes like his friend. He couldn't even remember when it had started to shut.

Holmes glanced at him.

"Now, John, you shall see what has both brought and what has wrought this desire in me to gift the dress."

A petite woman climbed out of the rude door shutting off the shelter. She was dressed n rags that barely clung to her thin body. But even though she was a ragamuffin in appearance, her eyes s hone like sparkling diamonds with an inner light rarely seen in any adult or child.

And if not for the dirt in her hair, it would have been the color of pure yellow silk and as bright and powerful as her magnetic eyes.

"Sherlock."

"Siren," he greeted in return.

She smiled at Watson. "A friend? Ah, the black bag."

She smiled even more broadly, the warmth of her smile enfolding Watson in its glory. "Therefore, you must be his very beloved companion, Doctor John Watson, that he speaks so highly of. I hope I didn't' embarrass you with my poor song."

Watson shook his head, wiping at tears in his eyes. "Madam, you have destroyed me utterly."

She looked distraught grabbing at her throat in dismay.

Watson smiled then. "No, no, no. Not that. With the utter beauty of your voice. I felt as if I had just been transported to the very halls of heaven itself and all my loved ones and all the good people of the world who had left already were gathered about me, comforting me, warming my soul."

She broke into tears.

Watson looked alarmed. "Oh drats! I've offended you!"

She shook her head. "Oh, no, no, no, no. A thousand times no. I never know what effect my song will have on others. I didn't mean to bring you grief."

"Not grief, lovely lady, but love and care."

And without thinking twice, Watson opened his arms and she went into them.

Even though she should have smelled horribly of discards, rags and filth, all he could smell was the perfume of angels. It was as if her very body were a fragrant perfume.

He glanced at Holmes,, who was smiling. "Thank you!"

Holmes just nodded.

"Holmes. Watson. Hurry we need you!"

Watson let go and turned to look as Constable Evans came running up.

"Drat it all, you two are the hardest blokes to find when you want to be lost."

Holmes waved him to a stop.

Constable Evans gave him a questioning look, then noticed the young woman that Watson still held about her shoulders.

"Constable Evans, I want you to meet the woman who shall one day be my wife."

Everyone, including the young woman gave Holmes a shocked look.

31 Gable Street

Inspector Bloodstone stood outside the building, impatiently tapping his right foot over and over on the sidewalk pavement as various constables rushed in and out of the building.

As Holmes and Watson neared from the other side of the street with Constable Evans in the lead, he turned and with a sigh of relief greeted them.

"About time."

Holmes nodded. "And good morning to you as well, Inspector Bloodstone!"

Immediately the Inspector felt like a complaining whelp and sighed unhappily. "Forgive me. I haven't slept a wink since the call on this case."

"Yes?"

"Inspector Bloodstone glanced about to make sure no reporters were near. "Very peculiar as such."

"As such?"

"You'll see." Inspector Bloodstone urged Constable Evans towards the entrance to the building.

He nodded and gestured to Holmes and Watson and rushed up the steps, taking several steps at a time.

"Ah, the vigor of youth!" Holmes noted as he followed.

Watson chuckled. "He's not that much younger than you."

"Not in physical years," Holmes replied.

Watson didn't disagree with him. Both of them had aged much over the last years from the various cases they had handled. From the Hollow Man to the more recent Zodiac Killer. Their cup always ran over and their plate was always full.

Unfortunately, not with sweet things, such as the scones that Watson loved so much, but with dark murders and foul creatures of the night. The worst being human beings who chose to leave their heart in the gutter as well as their morals.

"Come."

Watson nodded and followed Holmes up the stairs.

Flat 303 Gable Street

Holmes and Watson stood over the pair of bodies that lay on the sitting room floor.

A vase of fresh roses smiled from the table centered in the room. Fresh single vases of roses were strategically placed about the room. As a matter of fact, about the entire flat.

Holmes and Watson had examined every room and found the same signature. One rose. One vase. Blood red rose in all the vases.

"Fingerprints?" Holmes asked the Inspector, who stood silently in t he doorway to the flat, watching, his face drawn from fatigue and an existential sadness that always came over him at the sight of murder when it came to the very young,, who still had so many years ahead of them.

"We'll know on the morrow," Inspector Bloodstone replied.

Holmes gave him a surprised look.

Inspector Bloodstone shrugged. "Oh, there's prints, but they don't make a world of sense."

"Oh?"

"You'll see."

"Tomorrow?"

"Yes."

"Then you won't mind if Watson does his own round?"

"Not at all. I was hoping the two of you could come up with something more, or at least corroborate our findings."

"Very well."

Watson nodded to Holmes, and headed into the bedroom to begin there.

Holmes peered at the two bodies that lay across from each other between the richly appointed sofa and an Arthurian set of chairs which resembled mini thrones.

"Children?"

"Evidently."

"Where?"

The Inspector shrugged. "Another mystery."

"Which you'll answer tomorrow?"

"One can hope."

Holmes nodded.

He took out a measuring ribbon and began marking the shape and distance of the victims from each other and various parts of the room, noting down his numbers in a notebook he took out of his jacket.

Inspector Bloodstone turned to Constable Evans on a light tap to his shoulder.

"Son?"

"I heard the most beautiful voice earlier when I found Holmes and Watson."

"Oh?"

Constable Evans lowered his voice. "Holmes declared he is going to marry a woman of the alley."

"I beg your pardon!"

Too loud and too late to recall his words, he turned an eye on Holmes, who acted as if he hadn't heard a single word, but Inspector Bloodstone knew that was quite impossible. The man was uncanny with the way he picked up the slightest of whispers and intimations of dialogue.

He returned his attention to Constable Evans. "You're joking of course?"

"Most certainly am not."

"Your son has excellent hearing," Holmes told the Inspector as he rose and joined them.

Inspector Bloodstone blushed with embarrassment. "I'm sorry. I didn't mean to be so blunt!"

Holmes smiled. "It's hard to change one's nature without great effort."

The Inspector gave Holmes a piercing look. "I don't know whether to feel relieved or insulted."

Holmes looked away to where Watson was now going about the sitting room, gathering samples. He even placed one vase in his black bag after carefully wrapping it in a light linen cloth from his medical bag.

"Anything Watson?"

Watson turned to the Inspector as he finished dusting the last vase and impressing a print cloth against it to gather the fingerprints or markings.

"Pretty much nothing at this point."

He turned to the Inspector and carefully stepped over the hands that were holding each other, even in death's grip.

"Inspector, may I use your cold room to complete my investigation?"

"I was counting on it."

Watson looked once more at the dead couple on the floor.

"It appears as if they committed a mutual suicide."

Holmes arched an eyebrow questioningly. "Appearances can be drastically disappointing, dear Watson."

"Agreed."

Holmes k knew from the look in Watson's eyes that his friend understood completely the subtext of his statement.

"I will head out to the Cold Room while you arrange for our dinner later tonight."

Holmes smiled. "I was hoping you might say that."

Watson snorted. "As if there were ever a doubt in your mind."

Holmes chuckled.

Watson exited the flat with Constable Evans.

"Well?"

Holmes turned to the Inspector. "It would seem to be a mystery how these two died."

"Why do you say that? It's obvious to me that they had some kind of suicide pact, even if a bit on the...umm...bizarre side of things."

"I agree. But the obvious is not usually the issue; it's what's not obvious."

"Such as?"

"Motive."

Holmes glanced at the grandfather clock in the corner of the room. A red rose was wrapped about the large hour hand, freezing it in place on the hour of seven.

"Timing."

Then he glanced at the gap between the couple. "Distance."

Inspector Bloodstone remained silent. He knew Holmes was figuring it out in his head as he spoke. "And...more importantly...and herein lies the true mystery. Motive."

"I see."

"No, you do not. But that's no matter, Inspector, as we shall most certainly see quite clearly on the morrow."

"Why then?"

Holmes smiled. "Because you will have gathered all the witnesses I shall need to speak with to bring this case to a successful conclusion."

Holmes took out his notepad, which the Inspector thought he had been taking notes, but in fact was writing down descriptions and names. He handed the list to the Inspector, who glanced at it, his eyes widening in surprise.

"But how do you know both their parents are dead, they had a parrot, and a canary, and a horse and buggy at the Roamers Club?"

"Once you have summoned the ones I have listed, on the morrow we shall define the whys and wherefores of my method. Until then, good evening, Professor, I have a date."

Holmes left the room abruptly, leaving the Inspector with his mouth hanging open.

"A date?"

"Sherlock Holmes on a Date?"

He shook his head and eyed a constable who had been standing guard near the door, quietly listening and watching everything.

"Holmes never goes on a date," he told the constable. Emphatically. "Never!"

221B Baker Street

Professor Challenger let out a yowl of surprise when Conan check mated his king. "Blast it all, Conan, how did you manage to do that?"

Conan began rearranging the chess pieces, and preparing for a new game. "Because it's the only time I can best you is when you are not paying attention."

"I am so paying attention."

"I seriously doubt that, Challenger."

Conan glanced over at Watson and Mrs. Hudson who stood near the windows, constantly glancing out, as if expecting someone.

Then he noticed Harry Houdini, his tall slim figure, standing by the stair entrance, eyes that direction, unconsciously rolling an Ace of Spaces between one finger and the next, having the card vanish and then slide out of his left ear to his shoulder, where it bounced and flipped back into his fingers again to repeat the same process.

"I don't know whether to blame this mysterious date that Holmes is bringing here tonight, or my worry over the Queen being sick."

"Both."

Challenger sighed. "Both." He nodded and took the white pawn and started to move it.

"Uh-uh-uh! My turn." Conan moved his black pawn forward a square.

Watson chuckled. "Those two are like a man and wife sometimes."

"Don't let Conan hear that, John, he's quite enamored of his current one."

Watson laughed. "Admirable sense of humor, my dear."

"I wasn't joking."

Watson arched an eyebrow.

Mrs. Hudson laughed. "I was." She kissed him on the cheek and glanced out again. "Why are they so late I wonder?"

The sound of an old gasoline car backfiring outside.

"Ah-ha!" Challenger roared.

They glanced that way as Challenger took Conan's queen with his knight.

"You cheated!" Conan cried out angrily.

"I most certainly did not. You weren't paying attention."

"I most certainly was!"

"Then why did you let me lose?"

"I would never do such a thing!"

"Well you did!"

"Did not!"

Watson stepped over and gently slid the chess board away. "Gentlemen, I know you're as anxious as I to see Holmes and his bride to be, but enough is enough!"

He went back to sit by Mrs. Hudson again.

"Nice call, old chap," Harry congratulated Watson.

Conan and Challenger glared at him in annoyance.

"Ah!" Watson cried out.

He stood up as did Mrs. Hudson and headed for the stairs.

Baker Street

A beautiful new Ford Edison Tesla pulled up front. The car was about fifteen feet long and six wide, with two front and two back doors. It no longer had the huge overhead electric motor that last year's models did, but instead the electric motor was half hidden in the trunk area in back the car.

"No longer needs to be so bulky," Nikola had told Edison and he agreed.

"We'll put the trunk just below the doors. More room that way," Edison agreed.

The color of the car was midnight black with a metallic finish that made it glitter in the light upon it.

It had eight sets of headlights and sixteen in back about the motor and side fenders.

A large wrapround bumper not only held the engine secure, but allowed for a tow hitch or bar to be attached if necessary.

"Prepared or all occasions," Edison promised.

Thomas Edison climbed from the driver's side, revealing a plush red interior made from seaweed in a special process that Captain Nemo supplied to their factory for addition to cars.

"Look at that interior," Challenger cooed, drooling over the extravagance of it. "I bet it has a cigar compartment as well."

Conan nodded. "Tom told me the other day it also has a pipe well and one day it will also have raydeeoh.

"Radio?"

"Yes, based on that new fangled invention that Edison just put into the market."

"But that only plays records."

"Not for much longer evidently."

"Ahh."

Nikola Tesla climbed out the passenger side. He and Thomas waved at their viewers, then each went to one of the back doors and opened them.

Holmes stepped out and then his bride to be.

"Holmes!" Watson greeted.

Challenger and Conan peered from behind Mrs. Hudson.

"I can't see her," Conan complained.

"Open your eyes then!"

Harry stepped between them and clasped each by a shoulder.. "Please, let's not spoil Holmes arrival, shall we?"

Conan and Challenger shut up.

Harry smiled as the intended bride stepped around the car into view, holding onto Nikola Tesla's arm as she did so.

"She's beautiful!" Mrs. Hudson declared.

"Stunning!" Harry added.

"It's an actual woman," Conan observed.

Challenger snorted. "And you expected what a flask or a strand of hair? Come on, Conan, he's not a detective every hour of the day and night. Unlike the one you write about in your books."

"My Holmes is just more logical. It's not logical to have a bride when you're on such important missions of crime all the time."

"It's not a crime to love someone."

"No, but it's a crime to endanger them!" Conan insisted.

"Conan," Watson said, turning around to look him sternly in the face. "It's more of a crime to deny yourself what happiness our few years can give us. You should realize that more so than any of us having died once already!"

Conan lost his glare of anger. "I apologize."

"As well you should," Challenger agreed, leaving an open mouthed Conan fighting to find the appropriate response to his insult as Challenger rolled his eyes around in exasperation and hurried down the steps to greet the couple.

"Holmes,, who's the angel you have brought with you?"

Holmes starts to reply, then freezes at the sound of sirens.

Everyone turns to look.

Inspector Bloodstone is driven up by his son, Constable Evans.

"Holmes," he calls out from his open window.

Witherby and Cromb, Flat 209

Jim Fisher and his wife Cynthia are facing each other, pistol in their right hands.

"I hope you realize what you're doing," he tells her.

She doesn't waver. Her weapon remains trained on his chest. "I think not."

She smiles warmly. "And you?"

"Not one bit have I changed my opinion."

"That's too bad. Now I shall have to shoot you."

A loud knocking starts on their flat's front door.

Neither look that way or budge.

Both raises their weapons to fire.

"Say goodbye, Cnythia!"

"Say goodbye, Jim," she replies.

The front door shatters.

Holmes, Constable Evans, Watson and Inspector Bloodstone rush through.

"Police!"

Jim and Cynthia lower their weapons, a confused look on their faces. "Say what?" Jim asks. "Police who?"

Inspector Bloodstone nods to his son and Watson who take Jim and Cynthia in charge and head them for the front door.

221B Baker Street

"Quite. Remarkable!" Challenger declares, adjusting his bristling red mustache and drawing a hand through his thick beard a moment in thought.

Conan nods. "A mesmerist, you say, Holmes?"

"I do."

"What made you come to that conclusion?"

Holmes patted the hand of his fiancée, the girl from the alley, then rose to gather some materials from the fireplace mantle.

"This," he said as he laid down a flyer. "Is from Mysterio the Mesmerist."

He laid down a newspaper article. "This is an interview with the man."

Inspector Bloodstone eyed the clip a moment. "Same one we showed you."

"Yes, Inspector, but the one you showed me was today and this is from before the fatal shooting."

"Oh."

"Oh!"

"Yes. Quite the same attributes, wouldn't you say?"

Then Holmes laid down a single red rose on the table top.

"Beautiful!" Mrs. Hudson remarked as she entered the room with coffee and tea.

She set her tray down on a side table and reached for the rose.

Holmes stopped her. "Not yet."

He carefully lifted the red rose between two gloved fingers and then wiped the length of the stem of the rose and gave it to her.

She beamed at him.

"Oh! But you didn't have to clean it for me. I don't mind a bit of garden dirt."

"It wasn't dirt, my dear."

Holmes laid down a third piece of paper with chemical formulas on it.

"As you know I do some chemical work here in my bedroom from time to time."

And then he laid down the final piece of paper with similar formula on it. "This was committed by Watson after returning to the Cold Room for the autopsies."

Watson nodded. "Quite remarkable similarities if I do say so."

"So what does this all add up to?" Harry asked, coming into the room with a tray of steaming scones.

"Thank you, Harry dear," Mrs. Hudson greeted him and took the tray, then set it down on to the paperwork much to the Inspector's surprise.

Holmes chuckled. "Don't worry, Inspector, these are merely copies of the evidence. I would never dare risk the originals."

He sat down and Watson got up to help Mrs. Hudson distribute coffee cups and napkins, and then silverware.

Finished, they sat down side by side.

Inspector Bloodstone took a scone and sniffed it. "This is new, Mrs. Hudson."

"Made from my own garden."

"Oh?"

Watson smiled and gave her a kiss on the cheek. "I built her a dirt plot on our rooftop with her permission."

"As if you would have to ask, my dear John," she said with a loving smile creasing her face.

He leaned across and kissed her cheek. "All the same."

Holmes took his scone and then began slicing it into small nibbles, using his fork to stab each piece, dip it into is coffee, allow it to soak, and then consume it with one swallow.

Constable Evans nudged his father. "Ask."

Holmes looked over at him. "Ask what?"

"The woman you plan on marrying."

Holmes got a distant look on his face. "I'm sorry to say she had to return home this day."

"Oh?"

"You see her mother was quite insistent on it and Good Queen Mary didn't' want her angry with our sailors."

"What manner of woman has that much power and influence over our Good Queen Mary?" Inspector Bloodstone demanded a bit gruffly.

"Father!"

"Sorry, son, I just wasn't' aware she owed anything to any other principalities."

"Oh, she doesn't. Quite the contrary, which is why this woman's daughter was allowed to come and visit."

"But why would the daughter of a powerful dignitary allow her daughter to live in an alley of all places?"

Homes leaned forward and cupped his hand beneath his chin, then smiled. "Because she wanted to see if her daughter was ready to be with mortals as she once was."

"Once?"

"Yes. You see, her daughter is named after her mother."

"And what name is that, Holmes?"

"Circe."

A deathly silence falls.

Watson, the only one, besides Mrs. Hudson, seem unperturbed by the announcement.

Harry glanced over at Challenger and Conan, who were seated with jaws hanging down in shock.

Harry laughed. "Really, gentlemen, you couldn't tell she was special?"

"She was most beautiful," Challenger agreed, "But I'd hardly call that a reason to see her as otherwise exceptional."

"I agree," Conan joined in, pausing to reflect a moment on his next words. "But even so. Even if the daughter of Circe...which I grant is quite an astonishing event...especially to find her so unsafely ensconced in a nearby alley...why would we think her anything other than a quite beautiful personality?"

Homles chuckled.

"That's the effect she has on men, you know. That Circe has and had on sailors who tried to rape her and her followers."

"What effect?" Conan demanded.

Challenger grunted. "Of course, her voice."

"Exactly," Holmes replied. "Any who come within her sphere of influence as she speaks are at once mesmerized....which..."

He gently lifted pulled the paperwork from beneath the tray burying it, then pulled out the photo of Mysterio.

"Which is the final clue as to how I discovered who has committed the act of trespass which brought about the deaths of one couple, and almost a second."

Inspector Bloodstones face lit up. "Of course. We all k now that hypnotic suggestion is powerful enough to turn a man's personality into mud..."

"...But only if the victim is weak minded and willing," Constable Evans interjected enthusiastically.

"Yes. Exactly," Holmes agreed with a nod. "But this..."

He pulled out a small glass flask from his jacket, and set it upon the table. "...This is what we discovered removed any reluctance from the victims."

"What is it?"

"The Dust of Death."

Mrs. Hudson gasped. "Which is why you didn't want me to touch the rose stem."

"Exactly, dear Mrs. Hudson. Surely it would have brought no foul play upon you by any of us, but it would have made you quite suggestible and with that any stranger might have purposely or not have wrought great harm upon your free will."

Watson bristled with anger. "I would not have liked that!"

"Nor I!" Holmes agreed, then put the flask back in his pocket.

Inspector Bloodstone eyed that pocket.

"Don't worry, Inspector, you shall have this flask again properly back in the evidence locker where it belongs."

The Inspector sighed. "I only wish we could have nabbed the blaggart who started all of this."

"And I," Holmes agreed.

"I'm confused," Conan finally spoke up, no longer able to hide it. "What does the dust have to do with your beloved woman?"

"The daughter of Circe achieves the same result by the resonance of her voice with a very subtle chemical that is emitted when she sings. From her body."

"A pheromone, much like what a Queen Bee uses to drive her would be mates mad with desire," Watson pointed out.

"So you see, Conan. This foul Mysterio knew exactly what he was doing when he gave the two women and their partners a red rose each."

"He was seducing them into his control."

"Yes."

Holmes went to the windows overlooking Baker Street. "And I shall not rest until we find him."

"Because of the crimes he's committed?" Conan asked.

"That and also because..."

He turned about to face everyone. "He ruined my wedding announcement."

"Oh dear Sherlock," Mrs. Hudson sighed, got up and rushed to him to give him a hug.

He returned it briefly, then gently disengaged.

"I am fine, Mrs. Hudson. She will return."

"But when?"

Island of Circe

"When the time is right," Holmes replied.

Siren climbed from the small rowboat that had been launched to return her to the Emerald isles of Circe. The man who had been rowing it was blindfolded so the radiance shining from Circe and her loved ones wouldn't over power him. His ears were plugged with cotton to stop their melodic voices from driving him mad with desire.

Siren leaned back and touched his shoulder. "Tell Captain Nemo thanks for me."

"I will," replied Ned, Captain Nemo's First Mate.

Ned gave her that usual winning grin, with no idea of whether she saw it or not, then began pulling on the oars so that the boat turned slowly and then with a sense tuned by years of sea going he made his way back over the depths of the cove out to sea where the golden beauty of the Nautilus shone gloriously beneath the beautiful silver of the moon from above.

"Daughter!" Circe cried out, seeing Siren at the edge of the waters on the beach.

Siren turned about and burst into tears.

Circe clasped Siren to her bosom. "Don't worry, my child, you'll see him again.

"Will I?"

She pulled from her mother's embrace. "Will I?"

Circe didn't' reply.

Her eyes were focused on the mortal world and all the children on Earth to learn how to live as the truly special beings they were.

But beyond that, the worrisome all the free will choices possible.

Countless.

Mysterio

A very, very short man with a hat almost as tall as his own body, stood before a teaming audience of school children on the south of London. He held an armful of red roses beneath is left arm and an olive branch in the free hand.

His clothing was thick cotton dyed a royal blue with red and white cotton balls adorning the hems of his jacket, the lapels of his shirt and his pant hems.

When he walked, he didn't so much walk, as waddle like an overfed duck, or a fat swan barely able to move without flopping over.

But flop over he did not. He expertly aimed himself at the nearest of the children. A beautiful young brunette with sparkling brown eyes.

"Can I have one, ,Mister Mysterio?"

He smiled gently into her face. "You will love this with all your heart and pass it along to your father?"

"I will. I promise."

He gave it to her. Then gave her another. "And one for your mother as well."

She took the second one and the sparkle was lost from her eyes a moment.

He turned to the other kids in the classroom, grinned at the school teacher, a tall man with dark shadows beneath his eyes, who stood watching as if at a performance. Not speaking. Not even blinking.

Then Mysterio turned to the other children with a beaming smile, sensing the disappointment in their faces. "Don't worry, I have one for all of you. Even two if need be!"

The children all began jumping up and don happily, shouting for joy.

He began handing out the red roses, one by one, to the girls and boys, who all excitedly took one, letting out cries of happiness as they sniffed them.

The boys began fencing with them immediately.

"Now, now, you mustn't break them before your parents can have them," he warned. "That would ruin everything," he added with a smile that was vacant of any warmth and with eyes as cold as ice.

But none saw that and when they investigated his face, all they saw was a man who was jolly and fat, and everything nice.

MASTER OF MAGIC

"Previously titled Magic
And Illusions and with added material."

Transformation

S *ome years back.*
"Ladies and Gentlemen," Harry announced to the gathered audience in the Globe Theater, all of whom whose eyes were now frozen on his semi naked figure, which while not perfect, was evenly muscled and firmly packed with strength.

Harry ran every day early in the morning up and down the stairs of Scotland Yard, where constables would smile and greet him and then he would take a lap about the building, even passing arriving criminals being herded into the back area, where they would be booked and herded into awaiting cells.

So, he was not out of shape.

He even spent an hour each day, usually before bed, as it helped him to relax, lifting weights. How? He would donate his time to the local Home for the Elderly, where he would lug the heavy crates of donated food up and down the five sets of stairs from the basement to the kitchen area.

Everyone there knew him, because he always performed a magic show for the older ones every holiday and arrived on Christmas morning to hand out special gifts, he made himself. He loved to carve fresh wood into mythological creatures.

Each gift he handed out he would tell a short tell about the creature and its history.

But this night he was not doing that, he was preparing to launch himself headfirst into a flaming tank of burning oil and water.

He had never performed this trick before.

It was risky because if he remained in the water too long, the heat from the burning oil would soon boil him along with the water and if he didn't break free from the cuffs locking his hands behind his back, he would surely die of suffocation and drown if the boiling water hadn't already finished him first.

So, he was motivated to do well.

Highly motivated.

Harry continued, "Tonight I shall perform the most horrific and dangerous magic stunt I have ever created. I call it the Burning Boiling Doom!"

Everyone gasped in the theater.

Only the rustling of mugs of mead, hot potatoes being crunched between lips and the sucking in of breath by those fearful for him could be heard.

Some of the ladies in front were very openly dangling their handkerchiefs in a certain way to gain his attention, hoping that after the show, he would find them and with their handkerchief return to them that which they wanted, which was not the cloth, but his affection.

Harry, still being young and hormonally driven at times, would sometimes take them up on their offers. Even as he had the night before, which explained why he didn't feel his normal bright eyed, bushy tailed self this evening.

He saw one fall and nodded to the damsel. It was Mina, the love of his life and the bane of his life. He had never loved a woman so terribly strong and at the same time been so horribly conflicted in his feelings.

Loving a vampire is not easy, especially when their father is the King of Vampires, Count Dracula. But so far, they had kept their tryst a secret from him. He dreaded what would happen if they did not. He had this terrible fear of fang sinking into his throat and sucking his life away.

He had no reason to bring dishonor to the Count. So far, they only spent hours together talking. Always talking and talking. And for a young man like himself, with so many opportunities to not...talk, it was a rare and precious thing indeed.

Without further word, he glanced across his vast theater filled audience, nodded to William Shakespeare who sat in the top balcony with the Good Queen Mary of Scots, and then began climbing to the top of the large cylindrical bottle he would become immersed in. Once upside down, the only way out was for him to be uncuffing himself, twist about and fly to the surface and hurl him out onto the platform to save him.

He smiled. Let them think that. He had other plans. Then he lost his arrogant smile. If they worked.

He waited until the house constable, a young man with flaming red hair and a mischievous twinkle to his eyes latched the cuffs onto his wrists behind his back.

"Thank you, Constable Evans," he said.

Constable Evans nodded. "God's luck to you, Harry."

"Oh, I'll need that and more," Harry snorted with a smile on his lips.

Constable Evans stepped back and crossed his arms to wait for Harry to escape into his arms.

They were both to be disappointed.

Harry descended headfirst into the cylinder of water. It was cold. He had requested that to offset the initial heat of the burning oil on top.

An assistant dressed in the appropriately excited costume of brilliant reds and golds stepped forward with a lit torch.

Constable Evans nodded to her. She smiled at him.

They had a dinner afterwards.

Then she turned and flung the torch into the water.

Immediately it flared to life as the oil caught fire.

The audience gasped in fear.

The tension had started to build.

The assistant turned to the audience. "Mister Houdini will have but two minutes to escape the Burning Boiling Doom or perish!"

Gentleman up and down the aisles and in the booths above took out pocket watches to time the seconds and minutes, glancing at Harry as he hung upside down in the water.

The assistant announced. "The cuffs that the good Constable Evans has placed on Mister Houdini have no key for them. They cannot be unlocked by any pick or piece of metal known to man."

Constable Evans nodded to her after glancing at his watch.

"Sixty seconds left! The assistant announced.

Awakening of Magic

Of rain and shine
Morning and night
Wet and Cold
Hot and soothing,
The world is not awry.
It is really quite sly.
With the course of wonders
That it awards us.
—Doctor John Watson
Many years back.

It was a dark and dreary night.

Isn't it usually when everything you planned goes completely awry?

Slices of sizzling bolts of electricity arced across the skies and struck the earth, gouging and pounding it like a butcher tenderizing meat to be eaten. Except that for Harry, it was his body that was threatened to become meat.

He ran as fast as his youthful feet would carry him through the Golden Woods, ignoring the faces buried in the overhanging canopies of leaves and moss from the thickly clustered trees that carved themselves into the hillside he ran about. Crunching wood beneath his feet startled him because he wasn't expecting it and he almost fell when the fallen bark turned into fallen branches of larger and large sizes that stuck, prodded, and poked at him, grasping for his ankles and legs in attempts to hold him back and slow him down.

But he wasn't going to be discouraged by the constant challenges. He was not one to give up easily, or to shirk difficulties that might arise. He had learned from early on that anything tough enough to defeat you was also challenge enough to strive and overcome.

He recovered his balance, stifled a threatening sob, and clutching his rains slicked fists continued to pound towards his goal. A cave.

And not just any cave.

The fabled Crystal Caves of Merlin.

Fabled, because none had found them prior to his accidental discovery; and fabled because even though Merlin was still a strong presence in the new

Britains, he was still considered a thing of magic, and even though magic was rising once more in the realms, it was feared greatly because of the consequent parallel growth of evil.

Slam!

A bolt of lightning struck a huge boulder that loomed out of the darkness to his right. Splinters of stone sliced through the leaf canopy, and one struck his right ear. He immediately cried out in pain and once more almost fell, but recovered, with a hand grabbing a bush next to him to right himself.

But as he grabbed it, he felt something move across his knuckles. He glanced that way and saw the nose of a bear.

He screamed.

The bear screamed.

Harry dashed away, driven by the force of terror as well as fear now.

But nothing pursued him.

No monster.

And certainly, no bear. It was smart enough to stay out of the rain, thunder and slicing bolts of lightning that ached to carve the unwary traveler into smoking heaps of burnt flesh.

Harry was not yet wise nor old enough to realize that it was only men you had to fear, that nature was never out to deliberately get you...to strike you down...to maim, rape or torture you as men have done through the ages and continue to do, much to the dismay of those they trespass.

"Butt up, Harry!" He whispered to himself as he continued his curve about the hill, showing yet again that though no old, nor necessarily that wise yet, still he was clever enough, smart enough to know what he wanted and to not give up.

Whenever things got tough, his father would slam his hand against Harry's bottom, not as hard as to hurt dreadfully, but enough to alert him to pay attention.

"Butt up, Harry! Life's your friend not your enemy!"

As Harry ran like the devil was after him, he remembered those words repeatedly. Because he was trying to keep up his morale. When he had begun the hike to the cave this morning, he hadn't realized how far the cave was. He wished now he had never searched through his Uncle's memoirs, then he would not be so foolishly dashing through a night of storm and thunder, lightning and God only knew what else yet remained in his path.

But as all nights of terror begin, they also must end.

Several yards ahead of Harry several bolts of lightning cut across the rain drenched skies and revealed a huge dark blot between several larger trees.

Transformation 2

Some years back.

Harry could feel the heat of the boiling water above him stretching out to grasp his ankles and feet. At this point it was no more than a brisk bath might be, but he knew in a matter of fifteen second or more, the heat would reach his chest and then his heart would begin to boil within it.

He would die.

He felt the solidity of the cuffs behind him. Carefully, he probed the locking mechanism from the outside, feeling its length, breadth, and depth with his fingers.

While the lock had no known key, it did have a mechanism to close and latch it. He had learned of this torture device from a Chinese scholar who described it as a favorite way that the Dark Wizards there used to torture victims. Promising freedom if they could release themselves in a certain amount of time.

They never did.

But Harry was not them. He was young, optimistic, and quite, quite clever.

Fourteen seconds left he told himself, feeling his lungs start to burn from holding his breath.

He continued to play with the lock, giving his audience as good a show as possible, but not so much that he would die. He had no intentions of meeting the good people on the other side of the Path of Light just yet.

The assistant above glanced at Constable Evans. He held up ten fingers two times.

She turned to the audience, who could see Harry now begin to squirm as if he were unable to free himself. His movements got more intense and worrisome.

Shakespeare's confection attendants sold everything they carried inside the theater and more as the theater goers ate voraciously to calm their agitated nerves and growing fear for Harry's life.

Constable Evans held up just ten fingers.

"Harry has only ten seconds of breath left," she announced. "And no more than five after that before he boils to death!" She announced in a fatal tone.

Constable Evans smiled back at her when she winked at him, but he was also getting worried. Harry had told him he'd have the cuffs off sooner than this. But he waited patiently. Harry had given him strict orders.

But as he thought that he glanced at the audience and saw a dark faced man standing there with a pair of handcuffs exactly like those of Harry's. The man gave Constable Evans a smile that made him think of only one thing: Harry had been tricked!

Crystal Caves of Merlin

Put your dreams
Where they belong
In hope
And in song.
Leave the real work
Of living
Where it belongs.
—Merlin

Many years back.

Harry burst through the several bushes that overhung and sided the cave opening, making the last several feet with a magnificent leap...of faith and strength.

For he didn't know at all what he was leaping into, only that he must.

Don't ask him now why, or then why, he just knew he must.

And several seconds later a huge bolt of lightning struck the path where he would have stood had he not made his last leap. The ground was torn up and exploded upwards, leaving a smoking crater.

Harry was cast to the rocky floor of the cave, his thick cotton shirt wet from rain and now smoking from the sudden flare of heat.

He remembered what his father had told him about fire and quickly rolled over and over until it was smothered. But when he sat up, his shoulder ached. He reached back and could tell that his long hair in the back was crisped by the blast of flames. Even the back of his neck was slightly burned.

Later, when he returned home, his father would do the butt warning again, but much harder and then he and his mother would both hug him, sobbing with relief that he was alive, having feared the storm had taken him away from them.

But for now, his thoughts were only on the sudden pain and discomfort of his body.

"Pain is just a thought, Harry," a voice whispered.

Harry staggered to his feet, still feeling weak and woozy from the fall and the blast. His ears rung from the intensity of it. But he knew what he must do.

He reached into his right pants pocket and took out a small leather pouch with matches in it. He took one out and struck it on the rough wall of the cave entrance.

It lit so brightly, he winced for a moment against it, and then turned slowly to reveal the cave better. And as he did, he spotted an antique lantern hanging on a carved hanger on the wall to the right of the entrance.

The lantern was one of those old kinds that have no glass and is carried like a bowl of soup. He went to it, but it was out of reach.

After all, he was only ten. And ten is still small for most boys and he was probably never going to be tall, as his father anyway. At least that's what he thought then, even if later it was to be proved otherwise.

He scouted the floor a bit and spotted a large rock. He yelped. The match had burned to his fingers. He tossed it away, the crouched to move the rock. It was very heavy, but by putting his back into it, he was able to gradually move it to the foot of the wall where the lantern hung.

He climbed onto the rock. It wobbled a bit from his weight but held. He reached up and was barely able to grasp the lantern.

It took him several long moments of tugging to remove it from its stone hanger, but he finally did and got a face full of some coarse liquid as reward.

It dribbled into his mouth, and he said, "Yuck!"

It tasted foul.

Then he realized what it was before he tossed the lantern away. It wasn't water, but oil. A thick one, truly, but serviceable to his needs.

He climbed down from the rock, set the lantern on top of it, and then fumbled into his pants again for the leather pouch of matches. He thanked God that he had the foresight to use a leather pouch, or they would surely have been so drenched by now that they wouldn't ignite, let alone burn steadily.

He struck a match against the cave wall and then lowered it towards the thick lantern oils. Amid them he spotted something dark. He used his other hand to plunge into the oil and found a thick wick. He pulled it from beneath the oil and then put the match to it.

The wick caught fire and burned fiercely a moment, almost blinding him, then settled to a pleasant steady burn.

"Well then," he uttered, absolutely pleased with himself.

Another thing he remembered at that moment was his father telling him, "You're special, Harry. You're not like the other children. God has plans for you."

At the time he frowned. Who was this God thing that his father kept bringing up? But now he knew his father was just showing him fatherly love and respect. Encouraging him.

How did he know that?

Because it's exactly what he did with his best friend, Challenger, an older kid, monstrously tall for his years. He was fiercely freckled and had long curly even more fierce hair that always got in his face and nostrils.

He was funny and bright at the same time.

He was the one who got Harry onto the tracks of the caves he was now in.

"Harry, kiddo," Challenger had told him with that roguish grin of his, "You want to do magic; you gotta go to its source!"

Even in those days Challenger was preparing to be the explorer he would become...the great adventurer who would one day bring a living dinosaur to London and almost get himself killed in the process.

Incident: Transformation Three

Some years back.

Harry suddenly realized the cuffs were not the ones that Constable Evans had originally planned to use on him. The mechanism was unforgiving and somehow unrelenting. It wouldn't budge.

He looked out, his face suddenly filled with terror.

The audience outside saw and gasped, rising to their feet as they thought he was about to boil to death and drown.

Harry shut his eyes and forced himself to relax. As he did so, he saw his mentor in his mind.

The man leaned on his tall staff and smiled at Harry.

"No door is shut, Harry, that you cannot find another to open," the man had told him.

Constable Evans flew down the platform stairs and ran screaming to the side stage. "An axe. Quickly an axe!"

He had to break Harry free before he was drowned or boiled. He had only a few seconds to do so.

A brilliant flare of light erupted behind him, causing the audience to gasp.

The man who had tricked Harry frowned and then fled the theater.

The great glass cylinder tipped over and spilled Harry and the flaming water across the stage.

Harry flopped over like a floundering fish, and then said in Latin, "Finis!"

The flames that were threatening to spread to the platform and to the audience in front flared a brilliant blue and vanished.

The water froze.

Harry slowly stood up and raised his hands over his back, the cuffs falling away to the floor.

He smiled triumphantly as what few of the audience who were yet seated jumped to their feet and erupted into a thunderous applause.

Constable Evans ran back with the axe and slid on the ice.

The audience gasped as Harry was now threatened by the out-of-control Constable with the axe in his hands.

At the last possible moment Constable Evans flung his axe safely aside and fell into Harry's outstretched arms.

Harry smiled into the startled constable's face. "We really got to stop meeting this way, Constable," he announced loudly.

This time Harry and Constable Evans were buried n flowers, candies, and handkerchiefs, from men and women as thunderous applause shook the very foundations of the Globe Theater.

Shakespeare ran up to the stage, clapping the entire way. He leaped onto the stage from the side stairs onto the apron, skirted the frozen water, grabbed Harry's right arm, and raised it up high in the air.

Harry winced. When he had contorted to free the cuffs at the last possible moment, he had to dislocate that shoulder and it still hurt from doing so.

"I give you Harry Houdini, Master Magician..."

The crowd went crazy again.

".... And..." Shakespeare continued. "...the greatest living Wizard since Merlin the Magician."

Harry was stunned.

Even the audience was stunned.

They all turned their heads upwards to see what Good Queen Mary of Scots thought of that announcement.

They didn't have long to think about it. She rose elegantly put her hands out over the balcony and began clapping long and loudly.

Harry's fame had now been firmly established.

But despite all that had happened to his benefit, as Merlin might have said, there was a thorn yet to be revealed.

The dark man who had tricked Constable Evans and...him!

He glanced about the theater, the man was long gone, but something inside of Harry, maybe his fear, maybe his intuition, told him he hadn't seen the last of that blaggart!

And then Shakespeare repeated what he said earlier, jarring Harry back to the present.

"I give you Master Magician, Harry Houdini, the greatest magician in the world!"

Harry smirked. Now that was pushing things a bit he thought, but allowed Shakespeare his words, because it was good for his business, and at this moment Harry only wanted the night to be over with.

He glanced over at Mina, who gave him an alluring smile.

Yes, he was ready to have the night over.

He smiled back, already thinking of the wonderful time they would be spending together after the show.

Then he frowned.

But if only it could always be that way.

Show business was...well, showing off. And even if he couldn't personally get behind it, he had a business manager he loved and a great staff that worked magic in their own personal ways to help him do his work on stage and create a profit for all of them.

Sometimes, he thought it a bit excessive...his wealth and fame. Yet, when he considered how many impoverished people, he was able to anonymously help through their struggles, the charities he benefited and encouraged, perhaps God's Grace unto him was not as excessive as he sometimes...when in overwhelm or exhaustion...felt to be the case.

So, Harry did what was expected of him, he took the praise and bowed repeatedly as the applause and roar of "Here, Here," thundered throughout the Globe Theater.

When it began to lighten, he did an extraordinary thing. And probably the thing that had driven Mina away from him for years.

He spoke up.

Loudly.

"Drinks are on me!" He shouted.

And they were.

One after the other.

Even as his assistants cleaned up the mess on stage, Shakespeare happily joined the growing crowd of men and women who stayed after the show to celebrate with Harry.

He had thought Mina would join him, but as she left, she had turned back, and he could see nothing but disappointment on her face.

And that had been the last he had seen of her for years.

Maybe if he had done something different, he would never have become what he was this day...a wizard of power and a showman of extraordinary talent. He never thought of himself in terms of great or wonderful, even when his billings for his shows were plastered all over the place with such heady and gaudy reminders to the public. And yet, he was billed as such. So perhaps there was some truth to it, even though his humility never allowed him the peace of mind to believe otherwise.

But tonight, even though he had managed to outshine all expectations of him.

He had become a hero.

Even so.

At this moment Harry felt a great sadness begin to edge over his heart. Perhaps fame was not worth so much if it meant losing the dearest part of your soul.

"Mina," he whispered to no one.

"Harry Houdini," a young woman's voice jerked him from his reverie.

She came up so close to him that her very large bosom brushed his chest. There was no shame in her eyes.

Maybe, had Mina stayed? No certainly, if she had stayed, things would have turned in a different direction, but she did not.

He looked into the young woman's eyes. "You're the one who dropped the pink handkerchief."

She looked down at her feet.

Which were now over his.

He smiled.

Perhaps this night wasn't a total loss, he thought to himself as he stooped to retrieve it and hand it to her.

Her smile promised him many things as she retrieved it from his hand, taking hold of it and his hand at the same time. "I hear the stars are quite beautiful from Astoria Park this time of night."

Astoria Park was near his home.

She gave him a slight nudge with her bosom, and he felt a rush of excitement.

"Would you care for a walk?" He asked, reaching his arm out.

"Most certainly."

Then he laughed. He was still half naked.

"After I dress, of course."

"I'd like nothing better," she said, leaving him no doubt as to what she meant or what her intentions were.

Discovery

Many years back.

Despite all the trepidation, fear, and memories of discouragement, or more likely in Harry's case, because of them...he proceeded to explore the unknown the dark depths of the cave he had wanted to explore: Merlin's Crystal Caves.

Legendary thought they were, they were still of the earth and thus lots of dirt, stone and other things that walked, whisked, flew, and clung.

He swept aside a large veil of spider moss, which grows from the ceiling down and is more like a tapestry than actual moss, even though it's quite spongy to the touch and when it gets moist from water, a bit slimy.

Getting past his initial disgust with the touch of the spider moss, he shoved it aside and stepped past the living tapestry and allowed it to fall behind him.

If it was dark before; it was now almost pitch black. Even Harry's incredible night vision was challenged by this.

The entrance to the cave, though well hidden, could never describe in any depth what was inside. While seemingly old, moldy, and cramped at first, as he walked more into it and the cave opened wider and wider, the magnificence of it began to hammer into his fears and wipe them away, like water washing dirt from a plate. Even with so much shadowy and hard to see in detail, he could see enough to feel like he had just walked from the earthy realms into that of Fairie, a world of beings who Merlin had caused to separate from mankind for the protection, not of mankind, but of Fairie.

While man was maturing as a species, he still, for the most part remained greedy and aggressive, and murdering when it came to treasure.

All these thoughts and more passed through Harry's mind as he ducked and dodged, slipped and climbed along the path, wary of sharp stones and slithering things, of which there were many...scorpions, hammerhead beetles, snails with magnificent eye stalks that glowed in the dark, as well as the usual suspects...bats that heard him coming and hated the disturbance so flung themselves at him, missing him by fractions of an inch as they passed overhead, making high pitched screaming sounds.

Even as a child he had to be careful not to strike his head on overhanging rocks, but he managed to get inside, deeper, and deeper. And the further he went the more awestruck he was.

Merlin had left markers along the way, evidently because some of the cave was quite dangerous. He knew that because he ignored the first marker and ended up at a dead end, but the second marker he avoided brought him to a sudden pitfall, which he started to tumble into, but only his quick reflexes and more than a ton of luck saved him from.

He had clung to the edge of the drop off, his right hand clutching the hard ridged edge, cutting into his palm painfully and truly regretting not trusting his intuition and the markers.

That had been a big lesson for him from day one, trust your intuition!

He had found his second handhold, then a foothold, but barely. He regained a foothold, but his hand slipped. He quickly slung his other hand up and caught hold, but at the price of slicing it pretty good. He could feel blood oozing along his wrist as he pulled himself upwards. That and something else!

That several feet he had dropped was covered with a living wall of insects. Slimy, nauseous insects.

Slugs!

I hate slugs, Harry thought to himself.

But he didn't let go. He hated death even more.

His nose and mouth scraped the disgusting things and several times some of them latched onto his face and began crawling up it.

Disgusting!

He had to spit one out that was attempting to crawl into his mouth and blow hard with both nostrils when one tried to enter his nasal passage.

But finally, after long painful seconds he had his first leg, then his second over the lip of the drop off. He would have lain there to recover his wits, but more of the slugs were crawling on his hands and several started to enter his open mouth as he gasped for air.

Even more disgusting!

Harry scrambled to his feet and hurriedly brushed off the other slugs on him.

Then he saw that the lantern was standing upright, just half its fluid gone. A miracle it hadn't spilled out.

That worried him, not the miracle, but the fact that half the liquid was gone. He'd used almost half to get this far. He didn't think he had enough to go further, let alone return.

He wasn't so sure how long it would last, but his curiosity finally got the better of him.

So here he was at a branch of the caves, and a clear marker to the right glows a luminescent green. And that would have been it, but there was also a marker on his left, also luminescent and bright, but a deep violent red that kept swirling with seeming menace.

Now what? He thought.

That's when he saw the writing in Latin on the wall in front of him. He held his lantern closer and read it out loud.

"Here be a choice for the man with little or no voice; choose the path you will follow or fall into a sleepy hollow in death's lost repose."

What in the world?

"Red is the passion for life of a man driven and green is the path less given. Make your choice and make it wise. For here becomes a man or one who is wise."

Disgusting. He thought again. Except they weren't slugs this time, but rhymes. And not just funny or melodious rhymes, but choices.

If he went further one of two things could happen.

Judging from his first mistake he felt intuitively that it could be fatal to make the wrong one, so he sat down and pondered the meaning of the words.

Then his lantern began to flicker frantically. "Oh no!" He cried out.

Then the lantern went dark.

Disgusting

What Path Lies Ahead?

Many years back.

He woke up with the back of his head aching, as well as his back and legs, which he had crossed over in his sitting position. Something he had learned from a Hindu his father knew. Was supposed to increase blood flow and relaxation.

He didn't know about the blood part of it, but he had just fallen asleep. So, the relaxation part worked.

He felt about him and then remembered where he was. His hand discovered the extinguished lantern. He felt for the wall behind him and then slowly rose, using it to steady him.

He wasn't afraid of the dark. Had he been, he would never have made this journey from the beginning. But now he was not only in the dark, but in a very dangerous series of caves, where one misstep could lead to certain death.

Why would Merlin live in such a place? Or more importantly, why would he leave it so dangerous?

Harry then saw the two glowing markers, but the words on the wall had changed.

"Choose the right path to freedom, the wrong path to certain death!"

After he finished muttering those words angrily to himself, he suddenly froze. Wait!

Merlin had left clear directions.

Without hesitation he chose the right path, where the red marker was. Not a marker of death, but of freedom.

He felt his way along the wall, making his way deeper into the cave, determined to see this through to the end.

As he did so, occasionally his hand would come across some kind of insect. He resisted the urge to scream, but instead did his best not to hurt any of them, thus making his journey even more difficult, even if more humanly kind. At least to the insects.

This would become a trademark of his personality in the future years. A man who cared even about the slightest of things in God's creation, though a bit arrogant when it came to his abilities at times, and a womanizer when he felt threatened or at a loss. All those at that time still lay far ahead of him. At that moment he just a child on a man's journey of self-discovery and exploration.

As he proceeded, he began to hear a soft singing, almost human, but not quite. It was utterly stunning and beautiful. If angels were made of stone, perhaps this is what their angelic voices would sound like.

Soon the voices grew louder, more insistent, almost urgent and then he took a hard turn and as he walked forward the passageway began to brighten, as if someone were dialing a flame up in a lantern.

Finally, it was so bright he had to shield his eyes with a hand to proceed further.

He peeked between his fingers and saw he had come into a vast chamber filled with rainbows. And not just any rainbows, but rainbows of unimaginable colors, ranging from red to blue, yellow to brown, golden to violet and all the shades between and more!

He stopped. His heart had been pounding with excitement, but now it seemed to freeze as he realized where he really and truly was. He had found Merlin's Crystal Caves. Really, really found them.

Gentleman to the Rescue

The Present.

Harry was strolling down Chapel, enjoying the cool breezes of autumn when he heard a young woman's cry for mercy. The voice sounded full of fear and something else. Something familiar.

Help he would've understood immediately, but mercy was confusing to him.

He almost waited too long to seek the source of the voice, but when it came again it was in great agony. He winced at his reluctance and ran, using his cane to further his running steps, almost like a jumping stick the kids used in the parks.

He reached the alley of suspicion and plunged into it, heedless of self-danger.

She stood against the right wall, a tall man leaning over her, clutching a cross in one hand made of pure silver. It shone as he pressed it into her delicate neck, eliciting a new cry for mercy.

"Never!" He laughed. "You are a foul demon, and I shall not stop until your flesh returns to the earth from which it came."

The young woman in a move of desperation flung a fist into his face, which he caught with his other hand, which was holding something globule.

She screamed as her hand burst into flames.

"Oh, dear God!" Harry cried out despite himself.

He didn't know for sure if the man was a villain or not, but anyone who inflicted pain for pleasure was not the sort of fellow he could side with.

He rushed forward with his cane thrust before him. "Unhand her, you beast!"

The man kept his cross pressed to her neck, which was beginning to smoke.

Her eyes rolled in pain, not even seeing Harry.

Harry's eyes narrowed.

"You will unhand her or pay the cost!"

The man laughed. "A mere lad such as you is but a fly on the wall of my life."

He moved his hand with the globule so fast that Harry couldn't move. The globule struck Harry on his chin and then tumbled to the pavement.

The man gave Harry a surprised look. "You're not one of t hem!"

"Oh, but if being one of them, means being one of you, I am most definitely one of them!"

Harry stabbed the man in his side with the tip of the cane with all his strength. The man uttered a cry of pain and turned away from the pinned woman to fight with Harry.

But Harry wasn't waiting for the man to strike back; he already had his left fist flying at the man's face.

The man grunted in pain as Harry's left connected with his jaw, sending him flying back against the wall next to the young woman.

She slid away from him, her left hand gripping her burnt neck and looked at Harry. "You would help a vampire?"

Harry gave her a surprised look, then a grin.

"I'd help the devil if he was as lovely and sweet as you, fair lady."

The man on the pavement swung his right hand out. Harry tried to grab it, but it wasn't an empty hand, it held a long blade. Harry recoiled in pain as the fallen man struck his left leg with the tip of the knife.

Harry winced in pain as the man swung again and made a new slice, but this time higher on Harry's thigh as the man regained his footing.

Harry swung his cane then with all his might at the man's head. He missed his head but struck the man's neck.

The man rolled away against the wall, clutching at his neck, and screaming in pain. He struggled to keep his feet as he backed away from Harry and the woman.

"You haven't seen the last of me!"

He ran off.

Harry smiled at the young woman. "Well, I certainly hope that's so, because next time I intend to dent his head quite thoroughly," Harry commented drily.

"You're brave," she told him.

Something about her face looked familiar.

He was about to ask who she was when he felt so faint, he could no longer stand on his feet. "I think I need to sit..."

Whatever clever words were about to breach Harry's lips subsided into a moan and he collapsed to the pavement and into a gentle oblivion of darkness.

Magic and Illusions

"Shhh. Not a sound!" He whispered, his voice echoing throughout the theater, which had been acoustically modified to bounce his voice from one area to the next, amplifying it until it vibrated the bones of the ears of everyone listening. That caused their very bodies to vibrate, as if a gentle massage were being applied, and calmed them.

He needed to calm them. His next stunt was dangerous, even for him. He thrived on danger, not reckless danger, but danger that involved him mastering a challenger, or taking on a challenge he had yet to face and grow from.

Harry Houdini was the consummate escape artist and magician. He used his various skills to manifest an act of such profound terror and awe that the audiences sat spellbound through every minute, every second of it, some of them even fainting from holding their breath too long. Others piling on the popcorn, candy, and teas that the vendors who moved silently throughout the theater and sold.

That very side job was what truly paid him, not the theater tickets. Most of that paid for his helpers, the light engineers, the stage workers, the ticket takers, the manager, and the rent of the theater. He owed it. It was named "Magic and Illusions" after the very acts that he produced throughout the year.

Since he was as likely to go on an adventure or assignment with his Baker Street friends, he had created a career that could be hot sparked at a moment's notice to create more income for him and his people relished the time off they had in between job assignments, as he didn't hold back on sharing the monies freely with them. There were no poor people working for him, at least not after they had been employed for a time.

He hated poverty and its lack of medicine, the snide remarks, the dark consequences of mixing in with those of more. He had endured all those things until he had built a career that was magnificent enough, he could rise from his own poverty and then begin to spread his own abundance around to alleviate the suffering of others.

While he was wealth in laymen terms, he was not onerously wealthy. He didn't have a home that was ten stories tall as some of the wealthiest did, nor have expensive imports and portraits painted by the greatest artists of his time. No, his home was a single-story dwelling with enough room to sleep in, plan his acts in… a cellar basement for that with two rooms for storage and invention…and four bedrooms, a dining room, a library, an exercise room, and a kitchen. It would seem like a lot to the very poor of London, but not to a middle-class citizen, of which he was not. He prided himself on the simpler abode, for he often had guests, so the extra three bedrooms were as likely as not to be filled with either family or friends, or both.

His near Baker Street friends such as Watson and Holmes came to visit, but rarely stayed, but some of those who lived under the sea such as Captain Nemo, or in the clouds like Wells and Verne, they would come and stay sometimes for weeks or even months if they had an adventure together in London.

It kept his life full and rewarding. He had no woman in his life, he didn't think it fair to involve them in the risks he constantly took on stage and in the battlefield of crime and adventure. Though he did have a sweetheart he saw infrequently, who someone kept true to him and steady in his affections, whom one day he just might settle down with and have little Houdini's.

He smiled at that as he clasped one muscular hand and arm after another on the rope and climbed into the gigantic bottle that looked like an enlarged wine bottle with a narrow neck he could only get through with great effort. This was the sale of his act this time. He would submerge himself within the well of water of the giant bottle, have three chains tied to his ankles and feet, five metal balls, and his hands padlocked behind his back so he couldn't work his personal magic.

Oh yes, he smiled. He could do REAL magic, but he preferred the stage magic for the excitement of it, keeping the more ethereal magic for his adventures with the Baker Street fellows, or the occasional research he would do in the Orients for little known magics and fantasy elements he could incorporate into his act.

He would only use real magic when his life or that of another was in danger. Though he and Conan would sometimes use it to defraud charlatan psychics and wizards who claimed powers they didn't to fill their bank accounts at the expense of those with broken hearts. They didn't bother the ones that read palms and predicted marriages, and such, for they never overcharged, but the ones who claimed to be just somewhat short of gods, they had to be accountable. One way or the other.

So, in the course of time and years of learning he and Conan had made many friends, saved many a poor soul the loss of their fortunes, and been scorned as heathens and worshippers of the devil by the very people who did so.

Harry laughed inwardly as he reached the top of the bottle and turned to face the crowd. He waved his hands as he delicately balanced on the edge of the bottle to the cheer of the crowd, then waited as his crew hefted the balls and chains to the top of the bottle, in preparation for plunging them into the warmer waters and then he as well.

Outwardly he exalted at the pleasure he brought the audience, but inwardly, he was a bit nervous, for he had seen an old enemy in the audience this night. One he had not seen perhaps for five years. Time had not been this man's friend. He had never been a looker before, but on this night, he looked as dark as a devil. And no doubt as malicious and dangerous as before. The last time they had met, the man had tried to stake him in the heart, mistaking Harry for a demon of the night...a vampire.

He laughed inwardly. Vampires were not demons, but modified humans with a touch of magic mixed into them from Elfish heritage.

Harry had ended up in the hospital for a month from the wound, which only the skilled hands of Doctor Watson and the dear Madame Curie had been able to preserve him.

He had discovered the whereabouts of the scoundrel, and then used his real magic to send him off to a side realm...a parallel world where his kind could prosper with fellows of a like mind. Some might call that cruel and unusual punishment, but he didn't think it was cruel to offer a man who had attempted to murder him because of his misguide religious beliefs a way to redeem himself. He had given the man a path back to their London, but only if he were to change his ways.

But tonight, as he looked out into the audience for the man, and remembering that look, he knew the man had not truly changed at all. This was unfortunate. For both him and Harry.

No matter. Each challenge on its own merits he thought as he slid into the water feet first, the balls and chains collapsing to the bottom of the bottom and pulling him to follow.

In moments bubbles of air began frothing to the surface of the bottle as he squeezed through by squeezing through its narrow neck. He would not be able to come out as easily, for the pressure of the water and its viscosity would cause his body to swell somewhat because of its warmth and he would have to painfully squeeze back out after unhinging his shoulder blades, which would cause him remarkable pain...at least until he moved them back into their proper orbits once more.

His crew corked the bottle with a jazzy looking cork that was sparkly and gorgeously decorated to offset the danger of what he was doing. For it was dangerous. Extremely.

He heard his announcer, Jacob Marley, tell the crowd. "From the moment we corked Harry Houdini into the bottle he will have only seventy seconds to escape the bottle. His ability to hold his breath is no more than seventy seconds.

We pray he shall prevail so we can all applaud him and come again for another night of thrills and chills in the House of Magic and Illusions."

Harry's cue had been spoken. He began twisting and pulling, unhinging his wrists so he could slide the padlocks from them. Once dropped, he carefully began to raise his feet one at a time and working on the balls and chains. There were three on each leg, so it took him another twenty seconds to do each leg. He had used fifteen seconds already for the announcement and removing the pad locks. He now had twenty seconds of air left and already he could feel his lungs straining to not let go what precious oxygen he had left and suck in the water for air instead.

Outside Jacob announced, "Nineteen seconds. Eighteen Seconds."

Harry kicked free the last of the balls and chains, straightened up and hinged his arms and legs properly again as he wriggled towards the cork to free it.

"Nine seconds. Eight seconds." Jacob's voice droned outside the bottle.

Harry smiled. Piece of cake. He lifted his hands and pummeled the cork. It had taken him five seconds last time, and he still had seven.

"Seven seconds."

Harry pummeled the cork again, but it didn't budge.

Must be the extra curry I had for breakfast this morning he thought to himself, then still smiling pummeled the cork again, even harder.

He could feel his lungs on the verge of exploding.

Spots were beginning to form before his eyes.

"Two seconds."

The cork wouldn't budge.

The crowd in the theater rose as one in horror, hands holding each other, clenched to mouths, looks of horror as Harry appeared to be unable to get free.

Harry started to panic. He was out of air.

The old enemy in the audience rose from his chair, a look of satisfaction on his face as he saw Harry's look of terror and his thrashing to get out.

"Good-bye, old friend." He muttered as he turned to leave.

As he did so he came face to face with Sherlock Holmes and Watson, behind them was Inspector Bloodstone.

Harry suddenly froze in the bottle, closed his eyes, then as effortlessly as a seal sliding through a hoop, stepped through the glass of the bottle onto the stage, his whole-body dripping water. He began gasping for air. His crew rushed forwards to drape him in warm cloth, and then lead him towards the backstage as the audience broke into thunderous applause.

"You are under arrest for the attempted murder of Master Magician and Illusionist, Harry Houdini." Inspector Bloodstone said sternly.

The old enemy snarled and broke free, running for the stage, drawing a pistol as he fled the law. "Die Harry! You foul heathen and offense to God!" He cried out and fired, the same time as Watson and Holmes fired their own weapons.

The old enemy snapped backwards, and then collapsed.

On the stage, Harry dropped the cloths about him, turned around smiling and revealed a smoking bullet in between his fingers.

The audience, thinking the death was staged, broke into thunderous applause, yelling and screaming their love for him.

Harry, however, was not happy. He had tried to save a soul and it hadn't worked. Some just would not change no matter how many chances they were given.

He dropped from the stage and felt his old enemy's throat for a pulse, then motioned to his helpers, who came down and covered him with cloths.

"Magic and Illusions." He uttered to the dead man. "That's all I am. Magic and Illusions. But you had life and breath. Now...not even that. May God have mercy on your soul."

He turned around and climbed back onto the stage to prepare for his next act. His friends had used his act to help him catch the man, but instead all had gone wrong. He had much to think about where he had gone wrong in his own actions, to allow this soul slip through into a self-made hell.

Sadly, he left the stage. Sadly, he went to his stage room to ponder the meaning of his life. Such was the life of Harry Houdini that night.

Baker Street

Harry was nodding off in the back of the taxi, his tired mind and weary soul lulled into sleep by the soft humming of its Tesla electric engine.

The car stopped.

The humming stopped.

He yawned, stretched, and opened his eyes.

"Home so soon?"

The driver looked back at him and grinned, showing a healthy pair of fangs.

"Dracula!"

The Count chuckled. "You were so worn down that you didn't even wake up when I replaced the driver with a healthy tip. This by the way also included the cost of this taxi, which I shall happily drive at times. It's kind of fun if you don't mind me saying so."

Harry looked through the back seat windows, confused by the buildings about him.

"Where are we?"

"Where you need to be, Harry!"

221B Baker Street

"Surprise!"

Harry blinked his eyes yet again in wonder and confusion. Was he having one of these waking dreams, where you were so tired that you became lost in the dreams?

Holmes stepped forward and took his cap and coat. "Please, Harry, do come in and make yourself at home."

Watson grinned from alongside Mrs. Hudson. "My darling Mary has made you the love of your life as a special treat."

Harry looked to the dining table, where Mina Dracula sat poised with a huge cake between her hands.

She smiled at Harry. "Actually, it was my idea. But Mrs. Hudson made it. I'm not so good with cooking as you know."

Harry finally realized he wasn't dreaming.

"Mina!"

He turned.

The Count stood behind him, grinning so much that his fangs hung out. "With my permission of course, providing you behave yourself."

Mina barked with laughter. "Father, that's like asking the sun to never shine again."

Professor Challenger rose from a couch near the fireplace with Conan and they stepped to join them at the door. "We loved your performance. It was spectacular."

Mina set the cake down and took Harry's hands in hers. "Harry, we were all there to support you."

Harry looked around in astonishment.

"Even I." Professor Langston agreed, materializing between Mina and Harry. He winked at Harry. Your father insisted I sit between you."

Harry laughed.

He entered fully and sat at the table and in a matter of minutes everyone had fresh hot scones and cups of tea and coffee to sip.

Dracula sipped a cup of hot pig's blood and when Mrs. Hudson wasn't looking, made a face, which Watson saw and laughed.

"What's so funny, John?" Mrs. Hudson asked, having not seen the Dracula make the face.

"I was just laughing at how wonderful our little party is."

Dracula rolled his eyes.

Even Holmes laughed this time.

But Harry didn't mind the nonsense; he was in heaven.

He sat next to Mina explaining his history with the dead man.

Soon, even Dracula was lost in thought and conversation. With Holmes, who had set up the usual chess board so they could play a game. He hadn't won a single game against the older man and was happy to continue trying to out game him, but thus far was having no difficulty in losing, which was refreshing to a man, who constantly won instead of losing.

Challenger and Conan returned by the fire.

Conan watched Holmes and Dracula conversing and playing chess. "Now why didn't I ever think of writing something like this?"

Challenger laughed. "Conan, one man can write many things; but he can't think of everything there is to write."

Conan smiled. But thought otherwise. But being close to Challenger, he said nothing further. He was content to shut his eyes and listen to Harry chuckle and laugh.

What had turned into a terrible and frustrating night for Harry had blossomed into something warm and friendly.

His eyes snapped open when Holmes rose and tapped his cup with a spoon loudly.

Everyone turned their attention to him.

He smiled at Harry and raised his cup in a toast. "To Harry Houdini, Master of Magic!"

The others rose with their own cups and touched them together and joined him. "To Harry Houdini, Master of Magic!"

Conan glanced over at Challenger. "Rings rather well for a title, don't you think?"

"Nah. I'd rather it were something like Master of Magic and Illusions."

Conan barked with laughter.

Harry blushed and joined the toast with his own toast. "And hers to all my friends of Baker Street!"

They joined him. "Cheers!"

AUTHOR'S NOTE

I've always had a great love for mystery and adventure. Starting with Agatha Christie's The Bat and ranging to Edgar Rice Burroughs Tarzan of the Apes and Jules Verne's Journey to the Center of the Earth.

It was only a short step between those three writers to run into Sir Arthur Conan Doyle and his wonderful Professor Challenger adventures.

I first read Sir Arthur Conan Doyle's wonderful spread of detective stories when I was still a child. I didn't own books, so I read them at the public library, or my school library. There was no Internet of Things, no Internet at all at the time. I was very into books as a child, always a loner of sorts. Even though I loved people, I was somehow always more in love with books. Call me bookworm then. Now bookworm writer. Maybe.

I went through the entire adult library in my hometown as a child, reading everything from fiction to non-fiction, science fiction to fantasy, and classic literature to modern. It didn't matter. It was words on paper. I loved the smell of books. Still do, even though I cater to electronic books currently.

This is all a back-story of sorts to give you an idea of why my Sherlock Holmes while based somewhat on the canon of Doyle, is nevertheless much more than that. What would be the point of repeating what's already been done?

No, rather I saw this writing experience as an opportunity to allow my imagination to romp in his playground but take elements from other famous authors and stories I've loved over the years.

There are copyright issues when it comes to living authors, so even though I'd love to play in their yards too, that is forbidden territory. So, I have contented myself to take my love of classic literature...Doyle, Verne, Wells, Dumas, Shakespeare and pour them into a mutual melting pot. Kind of a United States of Literature, so to speak.

Whereas the Sherlock Holmes of Sir Arthur Conan Doyle functions out of London, England in the Victorian period; mine exists in a parallel world where all the authors who have ever lived and all their characters are alive at the same time.

Therefore, if you see me including Houdini and Sherlock together, Challenger and Conan Doyle, it makes more sense if they were alive in that world and not this one.

As a person with a strong scientific background...I wrote a treatise on reaching other dimensions (parallel worlds) as an 8th grader, which my Physics teacher was knocked out about...I believe quite strongly in an unlimited universe, where an infinite number of parallel ones/dimensions exist at the same time.

When I was in India, I found that some there adhere to the belief that everything that man can do or imagine exists in a vast cosmic tapestry so that we do not so much physically exist, as mentally/spiritually move through that infinite tapestry, each choice we make...right or wrong...creating a branching point that we must follow, even though there were already an infinite number of other ones. Remarkably close to the parallel world/alternate dimension approach that many scientists are now coming to accept as a reality.

When I was a kid, the scientists barely believed in 4 dimensions...length, breadth, height, and time. Now as an adult there is talk of at least 9 known dimensions.

But getting back to my stories, what makes them relevant and different is that I can populate them with any science, any character, any famous figure, writer, artist, or whatever and they all fit! They fit because I created them. For fun. For pleasure. To be able to play on a field of dreams with no end in sight.

So, as you read my stories, dear reader, keep in mind that the Tesla car in my story is not Elon Musk's electric car, but a vehicle invented by collaboration between Thomas Edison and Nicolas Tesla in my invented world. It runs not by electricity as we know it, but by different energy discovered by Tesla.

In my world, Sherlock Holmes is not the first one of the stories, but one of several. Watson, likewise. Just as Spock was duplicated in the Star Trek series of movies to continue their worthy stories, so have I decided to include devices that will stimulate our imagination, take us to places we could never have gone before, and allow me to interject from time to time some of the wonderful insights I have been honored to receive as a maturing adult. So, death exists in my creation, but it has many permutations and outcomes. All exciting and mysterious.

Following this is a description of major characters, as well as items used exclusively in my Baker Street adventures.

2023 GLOSSARY OF BAKER STREET UNIVERSE

John Pirillo

Copyright 2023, John Pirillo

Back Story

One night, when I could not sleep, which was one of an endless stream of them created by the Pandemic and an internal struggle with relatives unconscious of their effect on my ability to sleep, I determined to discover as much information as I could on the many characters I present in my Baker Street Universe tales.

Needless to say, it would take many more pages, than I am presenting here in this book, to unfold the depths of all my characters. Yet, I knew that if I did not take the time when it was afforded to me, when would I take the time.

Therefore, to your good fortune, and my sad long nights of no sleep, I have been able to accumulate a small treasure of information on Sherlock Holmes and all he has encountered over the years I have written my special version of him.

I pray you will find as much joy in discovering all the treasure of information I have unraveled for your pleasure, as I did in doing so.

I will try to be more diligent in the future with my time...as little as it may be...to continue expanding this section of my book in order that those who gain joy from the revelations may continue to do so.

Most sincerely,
The Author,
John Pirillo

Arthur Conan Doyle

He was a British writer and physician, best known for creating the character of Sherlock Holmes, the famous detective who solved many mysteries with his logic and observation. He also wrote other stories in various genres, such as science fiction, fantasy, horror, and historical fiction. He was born in Edinburgh, Scotland, in 1859, and died in Crowborough, England, in 1930. He was a prolific and influential author, who inspired many other writers and artists. He was also interested in spiritualism and paranormal phenomena and claimed to have communicated with the dead. Some of his most famous works are: A Study in Scarlet, The Hound of the Baskervilles, The Lost World, and The White Company.

Captain Nemo

He was an Indian prince and a submarine captain, who explored the oceans with his vessel, the Nautilus. He was born in Bundelkhand, India, in 1820, and died in Dakkar Grotto, Faire, in 1897. He was a brilliant and adventurous man, who had a great passion for science and nature. He also had a dark and rebellious side, who hated imperialism and oppression. He waged a secret war against the British Empire and other colonial powers, using his submarine as a weapon. He also helped many oppressed people and creatures, such as the Indian rebels, the African slaves, and the giant squid. He was a friend and ally of Jules Verne, who wrote about his adventures and discoveries. He was also a friend and ally of Holmes and Watson, who helped him escape from his enemies and find refuge in Faire. Some of his most famous adventures are: Twenty Thousand Leagues Under the Sea, The Mysterious Island, The Adventure of the Nautilus, and The Adventure of the Dakkar Grotto. –

Constable Evans

He was a British policeman and soldier, who worked for Scotland Yard, the police force of London. He was born in London, England, in 1860, and died in London, England, in 1940. He was a brave and loyal man, who served his country and his city with honor and duty. He was also a skilled fighter and marksman, who used his gun and his fists to defend himself and others. He was a friend and colleague of Inspector Blackstone, who was his superior officer and mentor. He was also a friend and helper of Holmes and Watson, who respected him for his courage and honesty. Some of his most famous cases are: The Case of the Beryl Coronet, The Case of the Copper Kings, The Case of the Poison Belt, and The Case of the Land of Mist.

Count Dracula, the King of Vampires

He was a Transylvanian nobleman and a vampire lord, who terrorized Europe with his bloodlust and power. He was born in Sighisoara, Romania, in 1431, and died in London, England, in 1897. He was a cruel and cunning man, who had a long and dark history. He was also known as Vlad the Impaler, a ruthless prince who fought against the Ottoman Empire and impaled his enemies on stakes. He became a vampire after making a pact with the devil and gained immortality and supernatural abilities. He was an enemy and rival of Van Helsing, who hunted him down and killed him with a stake through his heart. He was also an enemy and rival of Holmes and Watson, who foiled his plans to create an army of vampires in London. Some of his most famous stories are Dracula, The Adventure of the Carfax Abbey, The Adventure of the Lucy Westenra, and The Adventure of the Final Problem. –

Doctor John Watson

He was a British doctor and writer, who was the loyal friend and companion of Sherlock Holmes. He was born in London, England, in 1852, and died in Sussex, England, in 1930. He was a brave and honest man, who served as a surgeon in the army during the Second Anglo-Afghan War. He met Holmes after being wounded and invalided back to London. He moved into 221B Baker Street with him and became his assistant and biographer. He narrated most of the stories about Holmes' adventures and cases. He also helped him fight against his enemies and protect his friends. He was married to Mary Morstan, who was also a secret agent for the Queen. Some of his most famous works are: The Sign of the Four, The Red-Headed League, The Final Problem, and The Adventure of the Empty House.

Good Queen Mary of Scots

She was a Scottish queen and a Catholic martyr, who was executed by her cousin, Queen Elizabeth I of England, for allegedly plotting to overthrow her. She was born in Linlithgow, Scotland, in 1542, and died in Fotheringhay, England, in 1587. She was a beautiful and charismatic woman, who had a tragic and turbulent life. She was married three times, to Francis II of France, Lord Darnley, and Earl of Bothwell, but none of them lasted or ended well. She was also involved in many wars and conflicts, such as the Rough Wooing, the Chaseabout Raid, and the Babington Plot. She was a friend and ally of the Queen of Faire, who supported her cause and sheltered her in her realm. She was also a friend and ally of Holmes and Watson, who helped her escape from prison and clear her name. Some of her most famous stories are: The Adventure of the Fotheringhay Castle, The Adventure of the Silver Locket, The Adventure of the Golden Rose, and The Adventure of the Lost Crown.

Harry Houdini

He was an American magician and escape artist, who amazed audiences with his daring and spectacular feats. He was born in Budapest, Hungary, in 1874, and died in Detroit, Michigan, in 1926. He was one of the most famous and influential performers of his time, who challenged himself to escape from various traps and restraints, such as handcuffs, chains, ropes, locks, boxes, water tanks, and even a straitjacket. He also exposed frauds and hoaxes that claimed to have supernatural powers or abilities. He was a friend and ally of Sherlock Holmes and John Watson, who helped them solve some cases involving magic and mystery. Some of his most famous acts are: The Chinese Water Torture Cell, The Milk Can Escape, The Mirror Challenge, and The Vanishing Elephant.

Herbert George Wells

He was a British writer and social critic, who wrote many novels and stories in various genres, such as science fiction, fantasy, horror, and history. He was born in Bromley, England, in 1866, and died in London, England, in 1946. He was a smart and progressive man, who had a great interest in science and society. He also had a bold and adventurous side, who liked to explore new ideas and possibilities. He wrote many books and articles that predicted or influenced many aspects of the future, such as technology, politics, culture, and war. He also wrote many books and articles that criticized or challenged many aspects of his present, such as imperialism, capitalism, religion, and class. He was a friend and ally of Sherlock Holmes and John Watson, who shared his curiosity and courage. He was also a friend and ally of Nikola Tesla and Jules Verne, who inspired him with their inventions and discoveries. Some of his most famous works are: The Time Machine, The War of the Worlds, The Invisible Man, and The Island of Dr. Moreau.

Jules Verne: He was a French writer and pioneer of science fiction, who wrote many novels and stories that explored the wonders and dangers of the world and beyond. He was born in Nantes, France, in 1828, and died in Amiens, France, in 1905. He was a curious and imaginative man, who had a great passion for adventure and discovery. He also had a realistic and scientific side, who based his stories on facts and research. He wrote many books and articles that depicted or inspired many aspects of exploration and innovation, such as travel, transportation, communication, and invention. He also wrote many books and articles that reflected or commented on many aspects of his society and culture, such as politics, economics, religion, and art. He was a friend and ally of Sherlock Holmes and John Watson, who admired him for his vision and creativity. He was also a friend and ally of Nikola Tesla and Herbert George Wells, who collaborated with him on some projects and stories. Some of his most famous works are: Twenty Thousand Leagues Under the Sea, Around the World in Eighty Days, Journey to the Center of the Earth, and From the Earth to the Moon.

Hyde

He was an alter ego and a manifestation of Dr. Jekyll, a British doctor and chemist, who created a potion that transformed him into a monstrous and evil being. He was born in London, England, in 1848, and died in London, England, in 1886. He was a violent and vicious man, who had no conscience or morality. He committed many crimes and atrocities, such as murder, robbery, and assault. He was an enemy and rival of Dr. Jekyll, who tried to control or destroy him. He was also an enemy and rival of Holmes and Watson, who investigated his crimes and uncovered his identity. Some of his most famous stories are: The Strange Case of Dr. Jekyll and Mr. Hyde, The Adventure of the Black Mailer, The Adventure of the Hyde Park Murderer, and The Adventure of the Final Problem. –

Inspector Blackstone

He was a British policeman and detective, who worked for Scotland Yard, the police force of London. He was born in London, England, in 1840, and died in London, England, in 1920. He was a smart and experienced man, who solved many crimes and cases with his logic and intuition. He was also a fair and just man, who enforced the law with respect and compassion. He was a friend and mentor of Constable Evans, who was his subordinate officer and protégé. He was also a friend and collaborator of Holmes and Watson, who admired him for his intelligence and professionalism. Some of his most famous cases are: The Case of the Blue Carbuncle, The Case of the Copper

James Moriarty

He was a British mathematician and criminal mastermind, who orchestrated many crimes and conspiracies in London and beyond. He was born in London, England, in 1847, and died in Switzerland, in 1891. He was a cunning and ruthless man, who had a vast intellect and a twisted mind. He also had a vast network of minions and associates, such as Sebastian Moran, Irene Adler, Colonel Moran, and Charles Augustus Milverton. He was an enemy and rival of Sherlock Holmes, who foiled many of his schemes and plans. He was also an enemy and rival of the Queen, who opposed his ambitions and plots. He was also an enemy and rival of Lord Graystone and Lady Shareen, who resisted his attacks and invasions. Some of his most famous schemes are: The Red-Headed League, The Valley of Fear, The Adventure of the Final Problem, and The Adventure of the Copper Cannon. –

Jules Verne

He was a French writer and pioneer of science fiction, who wrote many novels and stories that explored the wonders and dangers of the world and beyond. He was born in Nantes, France, in 1828, and died in Amiens, France, in 1905. He was a curious and imaginative man, who had a great passion for adventure and discovery. He also had a realistic and scientific side, who based his stories on facts and research. He wrote many books and articles that depicted or inspired many aspects of exploration and innovation, such as travel, transportation, communication, and invention. He also wrote many books and articles that reflected or commented on many aspects of his society and culture, such as politics, economics, religion, and art. He was a friend and ally of Sherlock Holmes and John Watson, who admired him for his vision and creativity. He was also a friend and ally of Nikola Tesla and Herbert George Wells, who collaborated with him on some projects and stories. Some of his most famous works are: Twenty Thousand Leagues Under the Sea, Around the World in Eighty Days, Journey to the Center of the Earth, and From the Earth to the Moon.

King Arthur

He was a British king and the ruler of Camelot, the legendary kingdom where justice and chivalry prevailed. He was born in Tintagel, UK, in 500 AD, and died in Avalon, Faire, in 600 AD. He was a noble and brave man, who had a great sense of honor and duty. He also had a great skill and charisma, who inspired loyalty and admiration. He wielded Excalibur, the magical sword that made him king. He also led the Knights of the Round Table, a group of noble warriors who followed his code of conduct. He fought against many enemies, such as Morgana le Fay, Mordred, and the Saxons. He was a friend and pupil of Merlin the Magician, who guided him with his magic and wisdom. He was also a friend and ally of the Queen of Faire, who supported him with her magic and love. Some of his most famous stories are: Le Morte d'Arthur, The Adventure of the Sword in the Stone, The Adventure of the Holy Grail, and The Adventure of the Final Battle. –

Lady Shareen

She was a fairy queen and consort of Lord Graystone, who was the ruler of the Silver Forest, a realm of Faire where many elves, fairies, and other magical beings dwelt. She was born in Faire, in 1520, and died in Faire, in 2020. She was a graceful and charming woman, who enchanted everyone with her beauty and charisma. She was also a powerful magician and healer, who used her magic to help and heal others. She was married to Lord Graystone, who was her mate and lord, a wise and noble elf king. They were both old friends of Ms. Hudson, who helped them in the past with various matters. They were also friends and allies of Holmes and Watson, who shared their passion for adventure and mystery. Some of their most famous adventures are: The Adventure of the Silver Forest, The Adventure of the China Seas, The Adventure of the Copper Cannon, and The Adventure of the Lost World.

Lord Graystone

He was an elf lord and ruler of the Silver Forest, a realm of Faire where many elves, fairies, and other magical beings dwelt. He was born in Faire, in 1500, and died in Faire, in 2000. He was a wise and noble man, who governed his realm with justice and compassion. He was also a skilled warrior and diplomat, who defended his realm from enemies and negotiated with allies. He was married to Lady Shareen, who was his mate and consort, a beautiful and powerful fairy queen. They were both old friends of MS Hudson, who helped them in the past with various matters. They were also friends and allies of Holmes and Watson, who shared their passion for adventure and mystery. Some of their most famous adventures are: The Adventure of the Silver Forest, The Adventure of the China Seas, The Adventure of the Copper Cannon, and The Adventure of the Lost World.

Magic

It is a natural phenomenon and ability that can be used to manipulate reality or create effects. It is present in both London and Faire, but more prevalent and powerful in Faire. It can be used for good or evil purposes, depending on the user's intention and morality. It can be accessed or activated by various means, such as words, gestures, objects, or emotions. It can also have various forms or types, such as elemental magic, enchantment magic, illusion magic, or healing magic. It can also have various rules or limitations, such as cost, duration, or backlash. It is a source of wonder and mystery for many people and creatures. It is also a source of conflict and danger for some people and creatures. –

Hello, this is Bing. I am happy to write a page on each of the following personalities featured in literature and my stories:

Martha Mary Hudson

She was a British landlady and spy, who owned the house at 221B Baker Street, where Holmes and Watson lived. She was born in London, England, in 1835, and died in London, England, in 1915. She was a kind and generous woman, who cared for her tenants and their guests. She was also a secret agent for the Queen, who used her connections and influence to gather information and resources for her missions. She was well-versed in the affairs of both London and Faire and had many friends and allies in both worlds. She was a friend and mentor of Lord Graystone and Lady Shareen, who were rulers of the Silver Forest, a realm of Faire where many elves, fairies, and other magical beings dwelt. She also helped them in the past with various matters. Some of her most famous deeds are: The Case of the Copper Kings, The Case of the Poison Belt, The Case of the Land of Mist, and The Case of the Lost World.

Merlin the Magician

He was a legendary wizard and adviser to King Arthur, the ruler of Camelot and the leader of the Knights of the Round Table. He was born in Wales, UK, in 500 AD, and died in Avalon, Faire, in 600 AD. He was a wise and powerful man, who had a great knowledge of magic and prophecy. He also had a mysterious and enigmatic personality, who often acted in mysterious ways. He helped King Arthur to obtain Excalibur, the magical sword that made him king. He also helped him to fight against his enemies, such as Morgana le Fay, Mordred, and the Saxons. He was a friend and mentor of King Arthur, who guided him with his advice and counsel. He was also a friend and ally of the Queen of Faire, who shared his vision of peace and harmony. Some of his most famous stories are: Le Morte d'Arthur, The Adventure of the Sword in the Stone, The Adventure of the Holy Grail, and The Adventure of the Final Battle.

Nikola Tesla

He was a Serbian American inventor and engineer, who made many contributions to the fields of electricity, magnetism, radio, and wireless communication. He was born in Smiljan, Croatia, in 1856, and died in New York, USA, in 1943. He was a genius and a visionary, who had a remarkable imagination and creativity. He also had a mysterious and eccentric personality, who had many quirks and habits. He invented many devices and systems, such as the alternating current (AC) motor, the Tesla coil, the radio-controlled boat, the wireless power transmission, and the death ray. He also claimed to have invented or discovered many things that were never proven or verified, such as the earthquake machine, the free energy device, and the communication with aliens. He was a friend and ally of Sherlock Holmes and John Watson, who helped them solve some cases involving electricity and magnetism. He was also a friend and ally of Jules Verne and Herbert George Wells, who wrote about his inventions and discoveries. Some of his most famous stories are: The Adventure of the Electric Man, The Adventure of the Wireless Power, The Adventure of the Death Ray, and The Adventure of the Lost Inventions.

Professor Challenger

Professor George Edward Challenger is a famous archaeologist and explorer, who has traveled to many exotic and dangerous places, such as the Lost World, the Poison Belt, and the Land of Mist. He is also a secret agent for the Queen, who uses his skills and gadgets to infiltrate enemy bases and gather information.

He is a tall and heavily muscled man, with a red beard and mustache that cover most of his face. He has a large head with a high forehead and a pair of piercing eyes. He has a loud and booming voice that can command attention and respect. He has a confident and assertive personality that can sometimes border on arrogance and stubbornness. He is not afraid to speak his mind or challenge anyone who disagrees with him.

He usually dresses in a suit and a hat, which he considers to be the proper attire for a gentleman. However, when he goes on his expeditions, he wears more practical and comfortable clothes, such as khaki pants, leather boots, and a safari jacket. He also carries a rifle, a revolver, a knife, and a bag of gadgets that he has invented or acquired from his travels.

He likes to eat hearty and spicy food, such as roast beef, curry, and cheese. He also likes to drink strong and hot beverages, such as coffee, tea, and whiskey. He dislikes bland and cold food and drinks, such as soup, salad, and water. He also dislikes smoking, as he thinks it is bad for his health.

He speaks English fluently, as well as several other languages that he has learned from his travels, such as French, Spanish, Portuguese, German, Arabic, and Swahili. He also knows some words and phrases from the languages of Faire, such as Elvish, Fairy, and Goblin. He has a rich and varied vocabulary that he uses to express his thoughts and opinions. He also likes to quote from literature and history to support his arguments or make his points.

He has a high level of education and intelligence that he has acquired from his studies and research. He has degrees in archaeology, anthropology, biology, chemistry, physics, engineering, and mathematics from various universities around the world. He has published many books and articles on his discoveries and theories in various fields of science and history. He has also received many awards and honors for his achievements and contributions to knowledge and society.

He is a friend and ally of Holmes and Watson, who share his passion for adventure and mystery. He is also a friend and mentor of Conan, who is his apprentice and companion. He is also a friend and colleague of Ms. Hudson, who is his contact and informant. He respects and admires them for their skills and talents.

He is an enemy and rival of Moriarty, who is his opposite in every way. He despises him for his crimes and schemes. He opposes him in every opportunity.

He is Professor Challenger: a man of science and action, a man of courage and curiosity, a man of wonder and wisdom.

Good Queen Mary of Scots: She was a Scottish queen and a Catholic martyr, who was executed by her cousin, Queen Elizabeth I of England, for allegedly plotting to overthrow her. She was born in Linlithgow, Scotland, in 1542, and died in Fotheringhay, England, in 1587. She was a beautiful and charismatic woman, who had a tragic and turbulent life. She was married three times, to Francis II of France, Lord Darnley, and Earl of Bothwell, but none of them lasted or ended well. She was also involved in many wars and conflicts, such as the Rough Wooing, the Chaseabout Raid, and the Babington Plot. She was a friend and ally of the Queen of Faire, who supported her cause and sheltered her in her realm. She was also a friend and ally of Holmes and Watson, who helped her escape from prison and clear her name. Some of her most famous stories are: The Adventure of the Fotheringhay Castle, The Adventure of the Silver Locket, The Adventure of the Golden Rose, and The Adventure of the Lost Crown.

Count Dracula, the King of Vampires: He was a Transylvanian nobleman and a vampire lord, who terrorized Europe with his bloodlust and power. He was born in Sighisoara, Romania, in 1431, and died in London, England, in 1897. He was a cruel and cunning man, who had a long and dark history. He was also known as Vlad the Impaler, a ruthless prince who fought against the Ottoman Empire and impaled his enemies on stakes. He became a vampire after making a pact with the devil and gained immortality and supernatural abilities. He was an enemy and rival of Van Helsing, who hunted him down and killed him with a stake through his heart. He was also an enemy and rival of Holmes and Watson, who foiled his plans to create an army of vampires in London. Some of his most famous stories are Dracula, The Adventure of the Carfax Abbey, The Adventure of the Lucy Westenra, and The Adventure of the Final Problem.

Professor Langston, the Invisible Man: He was an American scientist and inventor, who discovered a way to make himself invisible by altering his body's refractive index. He was born in New York, USA, in 1866, and died in London, England, in 1897. He was a brilliant and ambitious man, who had a great curiosity and a thirst for knowledge. He also had a dark and twisted side, who became corrupted by his invisibility and used it for evil purposes. He was an enemy and rival of Professor Challenger, who exposed his secrets and stopped his experiments. He was also an enemy and rival of Holmes and Watson, who tracked him down and captured him. Some of his most famous stories are: The Invisible Man, The Adventure of the Baker Street Irregulars, The Adventure of the Invisible Man, and The Adventure of the Reichenbach Falls.

Hyde: He was an alter ego and a manifestation of Dr. Jekyll, a British doctor and chemist, who created a potion that transformed him into a monstrous and evil being. He was born in London, England, in 1848, and died in London, England, in 1886. He was a violent and vicious man, who had no conscience or morality. He committed many crimes and atrocities, such as murder, robbery, and assault. He was an enemy and rival of Dr. Jekyll, who tried to control or destroy him. He was also an enemy and rival of Holmes and Watson, who investigated his crimes and uncovered his identity. Some of his most famous stories are: The Strange Case of Dr. Jekyll and Mr. Hyde, The Adventure of the Black Mailer, The Adventure of the Hyde Park Murderer, and The Adventure of the Final Problem.

Merlin the Magician: He was a legendary wizard and adviser to King Arthur, the ruler of Camelot and the leader of the Knights of the Round Table. He was born in Wales, UK, in 500 AD, and died in Avalon, Faire, in 600 AD. He was a wise and powerful man, who had a great knowledge of magic and prophecy. He also had a mysterious and enigmatic personality, who often acted in mysterious ways. He helped King Arthur to obtain Excalibur, the magical sword that made him king. He also helped him to fight against his enemies, such as Morgana le Fay, Mordred, and the Saxons. He was a friend and mentor of King Arthur, who guided him with his advice and counsel. He was also a friend and ally of the Queen of Faire, who shared his vision of peace and harmony. Some of his most famous stories are: Le Morte d'Arthur, The Adventure of the Sword in the Stone, The Adventure of the Holy Grail, and The Adventure of the Final Battle.

King Arthur: He was a British king and the ruler of Camelot, the legendary kingdom where justice and chivalry prevailed. He was born in Tintagel, UK, in 500 AD, and died in Avalon, Faire, in 600 AD. He was a noble and brave man, who had a great sense of honor and duty. He also had a great skill and charisma, who inspired loyalty and admiration. He wielded Excalibur, the magical sword that made him king. He also led the Knights of the Round Table, a group of noble warriors who followed his code of conduct. He fought against many enemies, such as Morgana le Fay, Mordred, and the Saxons. He was a friend and pupil of Merlin the Magician, who guided him with his magic and wisdom. He was also a friend and ally of the Queen of Faire, who supported him with her magic and love. Some of his most famous stories are: Le Morte d'Arthur, The Adventure of the Sword in the Stone, The Adventure of the Holy Grail, and The Adventure of the Final Battle.

James Moriarty: He was a British mathematician and criminal mastermind, who orchestrated many crimes and conspiracies in London and beyond. He was born in London, England, in 1847, and died in Switzerland, in 1891. He was a cunning and ruthless man, who had a vast intellect and a twisted mind. He also had a vast network of minions and associates, such as Sebastian Moran, Irene Adler, Colonel Moran, and Charles Augustus Milverton. He was an enemy and rival of Sherlock Holmes, who foiled many of his schemes and plans. He was also an enemy and rival of the Queen, who opposed his ambitions and plots. He was also an enemy and rival of Lord Graystone and Lady Shareen, who resisted his attacks and invasions. Some of his most famous schemes are: The Red-Headed League, The Valley of Fear, The Adventure of the Final Problem, and The Adventure of the Copper Cannon.

Captain Nemo: He was an Indian prince and a submarine captain, who explored the oceans with his vessel, the Nautilus. He was born in Bundelkhand, India, in 1820, and died in Dakkar Grotto, Faire, in 1897. He was a brilliant and adventurous man, who had a great passion for science and nature. He also had a dark and rebellious side, who hated imperialism and oppression. He waged a secret war against the British Empire and other colonial powers, using his submarine as a weapon. He also helped many oppressed people and creatures, such as the Indian rebels, the African slaves, and the giant squid. He was a friend and ally of Jules Verne, who wrote about his adventures and discoveries. He was also a friend and ally of Holmes and Watson, who helped him escape from his enemies and find refuge in Faire. Some of his most famous adventures are: Twenty Thousand Leagues Under the Sea, The Mysterious Island, The Adventure of the Nautilus, and The Adventure of the Dakkar Grotto.

Magic: It is a natural phenomenon and ability that can be used to manipulate reality or create effects. It is present in both London and Faire, but more prevalent and powerful in Faire. It can be used for good or evil purposes, depending on the user's intention and morality. It can be accessed or activated by various means, such as words, gestures, objects, or emotions. It can also have various forms or types, such as elemental magic, enchantment magic, illusion magic, or healing magic. It can also have various rules or limitations, such as cost, duration, or backlash. It is a source of wonder and mystery for many people and creatures. It is also a source of conflict and danger for some people and creatures.

Faire: It is an alternate dimension or world that exists parallel to London. It is a realm where magic is abundant and powerful. It is also a realm where many mythical beings and creatures live, such as elves, fairies, goblins, dragons, unicorns, mermaids, etc. It is divided into several regions or kingdoms, each with its own ruler and culture. Some of these regions or kingdoms are the Silver Forest, ruled by Lord Graystone and Lady Shareen; the Golden Desert, ruled by King Solomon and Queen Sheba; the Crystal Lake, ruled by King Triton and Queen Amphitrite; etc. It is connected to London.

Professor Langston, the Invisible Man

He was an American scientist and inventor, who discovered a way to make himself invisible by altering his body's refractive index. He was born in New York, USA, in 1866, and died in London, England, in 1897. He was a brilliant and ambitious man, who had a great curiosity and a thirst for knowledge. He also had a dark and twisted side, who became corrupted by his invisibility and used it for evil purposes. He was an enemy and rival of Professor Challenger, who exposed his secrets and stopped his experiments. He was also an enemy and rival of Holmes and Watson, who tracked him down and captured him. Some of his most famous stories are: The Invisible Man, The Adventure of the Baker Street Irregulars, The Adventure of the Invisible Man, and The Adventure of the Reichenbach Falls. –

Professor Moriarty

He was a British criminal mastermind and genius, who orchestrated many crimes and conspiracies in London and beyond. He was born in London, England, in 1847, and died in Switzerland, in 1891. He was a cunning and ruthless man, who had a vast intellect and a twisted mind. He also had a vast network of minions and associates, such as Sebastian Moran, Irene Adler, Colonel Moran, and Charles Augustus Milverton. He was an enemy and rival of Sherlock Holmes, who foiled many of his schemes and plans. He was also an enemy and rival of the Queen, who opposed his ambitions and plots. He was also an enemy and rival of Lord Graystone and Lady Shareen, who resisted his attacks and invasions. Some of his most famous schemes are: The Red-Headed League, The Valley of Fear, The Adventure of the Final Problem, and The Adventure of the Copper Cannon.

Sherlock Holmes

He was a British detective and consultant, who solved many mysteries and cases with his logic and observation. He was born in London, England, in 1854, and died in Sussex, England, in 1932. He was a brilliant and eccentric man, who had a keen eye for detail and a remarkable memory. He also had a wide range of knowledge and skills, such as chemistry, violin, martial arts, and disguise. He lived at 221B Baker Street with his friend and biographer, John Watson. He also had a network of informants and helpers, such as the Baker Street Irregulars, a group of street children who spied for him. He was a friend and ally of the Queen, who hired him for some of her secret missions. He was also a friend and ally of Lord Graystone and Lady Shareen, who were rulers of the Silver Forest, a realm of Faire where many elves, fairies, and other magical beings dwelt. He was an enemy and rival of Professor Moriarty, who was the mastermind behind many crimes and conspiracies in London and beyond. Some of his most famous cases are: The Hound of the Baskervilles, A Scandal in Bohemia, The Adventure of the Speckled Band, and The Final Problem.

Some of Moriarty's other minions

Sebastian Moran, who is Moriarty's right-hand man and chief assassin. He is an expert marksman and sniper, who can kill anyone with his rifle.

Irene Adler, who is Moriarty's lover and partner in crime. She is an opera singer and a master of disguise, who can seduce anyone with her voice and charm.

Colonel Moran, who is Moriarty's cousin and ally. He is an army officer and a smuggler, who can provide Moriarty with weapons and supplies.

Charles Augustus Milverton, who is Moriarty's associate and rival. He is a blackmailer and a spy, who can extort anyone with his secrets and information.

(Author's note. I have added the above for your enjoyment only, as I have not yet used any of the characters in any of my published books. I hope to, but time controls the measure of my creations, and not I.)

Steampunk Science

My version of England is a blend of the very dark and the lighter side of human existence.

On the one hand we have Harry Houdini and Merlin the Magician who exemplify the better nature of magic and its welders, and on the other hand we have the darker side as led by Lovecraft, Dorian Gray, Fu Manchu, and of course the ever well known, Professor Moriarty.

But I would be failing you entirely, if I did not also disclose the eminent presence of Steampunk Science in my books. Though it is not always quite as blatant as the scones of Doctor Watson, nevertheless, it is everywhere in the Baker Street Universe I have created.

From steam driven unicycles to tri-pellor blimps.

From the Master of the World to the humming car of Professor Challenger, an oversized electric car with an engine on its roof, which I am quite sure

General Motors and all present-day motor car manufacturers would have a hard time swallowing...for economical reasons, as well as tailorability, as they are not built to be as sleek and fun as current drivers in our world expect and deploy.

It is also interesting to note that I am also showing how the Baker Street Universe and Holmes's new London are at the dawn of recognizing the importance of balancing the ecology with environment.

This means steampunk science is at best a dinosaur, soon to be slain, just as...hopefully...our own destructive use of the ecology nears an end...either wonderfully...or more catastrophically as some predict.

The Copper Cannon

Works by using copper as its source of power. Copper is a metal that can conduct electricity and heat very well. The Copper Cannon has a large chamber where copper bars and wires are stored and heated by fire. The heat causes the copper to melt and form a liquid. The liquid copper is then pumped into a barrel, where it is compressed and accelerated by magnetic coils. The barrel has a nozzle at the end, where the liquid copper is ejected as a stream of molten metal. The stream of molten metal is then electrified by another set of coils, creating a powerful blast of electricity. The blast of electricity can travel through the air and hit any target within range, causing massive damage and destruction.

Request for Review

If you found some pleasure in reading my work, please take the time to leave a review for it. Authors can thrive or die for the lack of reviews.

Thanking you in advance for your kindness.

John

Author's Note

If you want to keep abreast of the latest news, follow me on my author site: www.bakerstreetuniverses.com

Connect with me on Twitter: @johnpirillo

Friend me at my Facebook page: John Pirillo, Author[1].

Join my Baker Street Universe group to get things I don't usually share with others, and to hash over the universe I've created with me and fellow authors and readers. I'll be having incredibly special giveaways, advance copies, and autographed work as well as other surprises to my friends who join me there.

My artwork is available at: https://john-pirillo.pixels.com/

---

1.   https://www.facebook.com/john.pirillo.3.

OTHER BOOKS BY THE AUTHOR

SHERLOCK HOLMES, MAMMOTH FANTASY, MURDER AND MYSTERY TALES 21

SHERLOCK HOLMES, MAMMOTH FANTASY, MURDER AND MYSTERY TALES 22

SHERLOCK HOLMES, MAMMOTH FANTASY, MURDER AND MYSTERY TALES 23

SHERLOCK HOLMES, MAMMOTH FANTASY, MURDER AND MYSTERY TALES 24

SHERLOCK HOLMES, MAMMOTH FANTASY, MURDER AND MYSTERY TALES 25

SHERLOCK HOLMES, MAMMOTH FANTASY, MURDER AND MYSTERY TALES 26

SHERLOCK HOLMES, MAMMOTH FANTASY, MURDER, AND MYSTERY TALES 27

SHERLOCK HOLMES, MAMMOTH FANTASY, MURDER, AND MYSTERY TALES 28

SHERLOCK HOLMES, MOST PECULIAR

SHIFTERS+

SHIFTERS2+

DOUBLE HOLMES 2

ABNOMALIES

BAKER STREET WIZARD

BAKER STREET WIZARD 2

BAKER STREET WIZARD 3

DEEP SILENCE

DOUBLE HOLMES

DOUBLE HOLMES 2

DOUBLE HOLMES 3

ALEXANDER DUMAS, THE SEA DEMON
SECRET ADVENTURES OF JULES VERNE AND
ALEXANDER DUMAS, HOLLOW EARTH
SHERLOCK HOLMES, BAKER STREET WIZARD
SHERLOCK HOLMES, BAKER STREET WIZARD 2
SHERLOCK HOLMES, BAKER STREET WIZARD 3
SHERLOCK HOLMES, BAKER STREET WIZARD 4
SHERLOCK HOLMES, BAKER STREET WIZARD 5
SHERLOCK HOLMES, BAKER STREET WIZARD 5
SHERLOCK HOLMES, BLACK WIZARD
SHERLOCK HOLMES, CURSE OF THE BLACK WIZARD
SHERLOCK HOLMES, DEADLY MASTER
SHERLOCK HOLMES, HALLOWEEN VAMPIRE TALES
SHERLOCK HOLMES, WEREWOLVE TALES
SHERLOCK HOLMES, HALLOWEEN MONSTERS
SHERLOCK HOLMES, HALLOWEEN MONSTERS 2
SHERLOCK HOLMES, LORD OF THE TREES
SHERLOCK HOLMES, THE BAKER STREET UNIVERSE
SHERLOCK HOLMES, URBAN FANTASY MYSTERIES
SHERLOCK HOLMES, URBAN FANTASY MYSTERIES 2
SHERLOCK HOLMES, URBAN FANTASY MYSTERIES 3
SHIFTER 1-4
THE CTHULHU INCIDENT 1-5

Don't miss out!

Visit the website below and you can sign up to receive emails whenever John Pirillo publishes a new book. There's no charge and no obligation.

https://books2read.com/r/B-A-EMSD-QNZQC

BOOKS 2 READ

Connecting independent readers to independent writers.

Did you love *Double Holmes 18*? Then you should read *Double Holmes 17*[2] by John Pirillo!

Two more great Sherlock Holmes mystery adventures.

THE TRAGIC DEATH OF SHERLOCK HOLMES

Can Watson deal with the body discovered in Switzerland?

One that appears to be that of Sherlock Holmes!

HARSH MEASURES

How can it be?

They are not human, but what they are made of is not only surprising, but horrifying!

Sit back, buckle up for another series of Sherlock Holmes tales!

Read more at www.johnpirillo.com.

---

2. https://books2read.com/u/3y6gBV

3. https://books2read.com/u/3y6gBV

Also by John Pirillo

Angel Hamilton
Broken Fangs

Baker Street Universe Tales
Baker Street Universe Tales
Baker Street Universe Tales 2
Baker Street Universe Tales 3
Baker Street Universe Tales 4
Baker Street Universe Tales 5
Baker Street Universe Tales 6
Baker Street Universe Tales Seven

BAKER STREET WIZARD
Baker Street Wizard 4
Baker Street Wizard 5

Between
Prince of Between

"Classic Baker Street Universe Sherlock Holmes"
Sherlock Holme: Hyde's Night of Terror
Case of the Deadly Goddess
Case of the Abominable

Cythulhu
The Cthulhu Incident
The Eye of Cthulhu
The Throne of Cythulhu
Throne of Cthulhu
Giants of Cythulhu

Deadly
Sherlock Holmes, Deadly Master
Sherlock Holmes, Deadly Magic

Detective Judge Dee
Detective Dee Murder Most Chaste

Double Holmes
Sherlock Holmes, Double Holmes 2
Double Holmes 7
Double Holmes 8
Double Holmes 9
Double Holmes 10
Double Holmes 11
Double Holmes 12

Infinite Tales
Infinite Tales
Infinite Tales Two

Monster Hunter
Monster Hunter

Mystery Knight
HellBound Mystery
Hell Bound Angel

PhaseShift
PhaseShift
PhaseShift Two: Crossover
PhaseShift: Shifting Worlds

Rocketman
Rocketman
Rocket Man, Time Streams
Rocketman Christmas
Time Wars
Arch of Time

Secret Adventures of Jules Verne and Alexander Dumas
Hollow Earth
Hollow Earth

Sherlock Holmes
Sherlock Holmes, ICE
The Ice Man
Sherlock Holmes Fallen
Sherlock Holmes: Monster
Sherlock Holmes: Tick Tock
Sherlock Holmes Christmas Magic
Sherlock Holmes Dark Secret
Sherlock Holmes Shadow of Dorian Gray
Sherlock Holmes Vampire
Sherlock Holmes: Cursed in Stone
Sherlock Holmes Apparition
Sherlock Holmes Case of the Raging Madness
Sherlock Holmes Dark Princess
Sherlock Holmes Dark Angel
Constable Evans' Fancy
Sherlock Holmes Matter of Perception
Sherlock Holmes Tangled
Sherlock Holmes Case of the Gossamer Lady
Sherlock Holmes House of Shadows
Sherlock Holmes The Yellow Death
Sherlock Holmes Oblique
Sherlock Holmes Mystery Train Winter Collection
Sherlock Holmes A Tale Less Told
Sherlock Holmes Mystery Six
Sherlock Holmes, Rules of Darkness, Special Edition
Sherlock Holmes Shape of Justice
Sherlock Holmes Christmas Magic
Sherlock Holmes Fallen Angel
Ghostly Shadows
Sherlock Holmes Bloody Hell
Sherlock Holmes Monster of the Tower
Sherlock Holmes Darkest of Nights

Sherlock Holmes Nightmare
Sherlock Holmes Poetry of Death
Sherlock Holmes, Dracula
Sherlock Holmes #3, Ice Storm
Sherlock Holmes, Baker Street Wizard 3

Sherlock Holmes Double Holmes
Sherlock Holmes, Double Holmes 1

Sherlock Holmes, Mammoth Fantasy, Murder and Mystery Tales
Sherlock Holmes, Mammoth Fantasy, Murder, and Mystery Tales 15
Sherlock Holmes Mammoth Fantasy, Murder, and Mystery Tales 17
Sherlock Holmes Mammoth Fantasy, Murder, and Mystery Tales 26
Sherlock Holmes Mammoth Fantasy, Murder, and Mystery Tales 14

Sherlock Holmes, Mammoth Fantasy, Murder, and Mystery Tales 15
Sherlock, Holmes, Mammoth Fantasy, Murder, and Mystery Tales 15

Sherlock Holmes Urban Fantasy Mysteries
Sherlock Holmes Urban Fantasy Mysteries
Sherlock Holmes, Halloween Monsters
Sherlock Holmes Urban Fantasy Mysteries 2
Sherlock Holmes Urban Fantasy Mysteries 3
Sherlock Holmes, Urban Fantasy Mysteries 3
Sherlock Holmes Urban Fantasy Mysteries 4
Sherlock Holmes, Artifact
Sherlock Holmes, The Dracula Files
Sherlock Holmes, Dark Clues
Sherlock Holmes, Case of the Undying Man

Sherlock Holmes, Mystery of the Sea
Sherlock Holmes, Night Watch
Sherlock Holmes, Mystery of the Path not Taken
Sherlock Holmes, the Dorian Gray Affair
The Baker Street Universe
Sherlock Holmes, The Dracula Affair
Spector
Sherlock Holmes, Rules of Darkness
Sherlock Holmes, A Tale Less Told
Sherlock Holmes, The Christmas Star
Sherlock Holmes, Christmas Tales
Steampunk Holmes
Sherlock HOlmes, Deadly Valentine's Day
Sherlock Holmes, Angel Murders
Sherlock Holmes, Deadly Intent
Sherlock Holmes, White Diamond Mystery
Sherlock Holmes, Gears World, Box Set One
Sherlock Holmes, The Blue Fire of Harry Houdini
Sherlock Holmes, White Diamond Vampire Mystery
Sherlock Holmes, Black Tower
Sherlock Holmes, Tales of the Macabre
Sherlock Holmes, Baker Street Wizard
Sherlock Holmes, Usher
Sherlock Holmes, Baker Street Wizard 2
Sherlock Holmes, Double Holmes 1
Sherlock Holmes, Cave of the Dark Elf
Sherlock Holmes, Something Wicked
Sherlock Holmes, Gears Word 3
Sherlock Holmes, Gears World 4
Sherlock Holmes, Deadly
Sherlock Holmes, Urban Fantasy Mysteries Six
Werewolves
Sherlock Holmes, Mammoth Fantasy, Murder, and Mystery Tales 27
Sherlock Holmes, Urban Fantasy Mysteries
Sherlock Holmes, Lord of the Trees

Sherlock Holmes, The Ghost Wars, Book One, Rise of the Ghost Empire

Sherlock Holmes, Urban Fantasy Mystery Tales
Sherlock Holmes, Urban Fantasy Mystery Tales 2
Sherlock Holmes, Dark Matters
Sherlock Holmes, Black Wizard
Sherlock Holmes, Curse of the Black Wizard
Sherlock Holmes, The Ghost Wars, Book Two: The War of Magic

Sky Captain Adventures
Sky Captain Adventures 2, Zombie World
Sky Captain Adventures 3
Sky Captain Adventures 4
Sky Captain Adventures Box Set

Steampunk Holmes
Sherlock Holmes, Gears of the Goddess

The Baker Street Detective
The Baker Street Detective 5, The Howling Wind
Strange Times, The Baker Street Detective, Book2
The Baker Street Detective, Hollow Man
Sherlock Holmes, Baker Street Detectives

Thrilling Mystery Tales
Thrilling Mystery Tales 2

Twist
Twist 2
Twister

Urban Fantasies
Urban Fantasies 1
Urban Fantasies 3
Urban Fantasies

War of the Worlds
Battle for Earth

WireShip
Wirestation Red Lion

Standalone
Sherlock Holmes Deadly Consequences
Invisibility Factor
Red Painted Souls
Between
Robin Hood
Shadow Man
The Rainbow Bridge
Cartoon, Johnnie Angel
Sherlock Holmes 221B
Sherlock Holmes Shape Shifter
Urban Fantasy Mysteries

Sherlock Holmes, Urban Fantasy Mysteries
Halloween Mysteries
Invasion
Romancing the Word
Romancing the Word Workbook
Sherlock Holmes, Gears World 2
Thrilling Mystery Tales
Weird Short Tales
Spectre Forces
Young King Arthur
Dark Midnight
Anomalies
Shifter+
Shifter 4+
Deep Silence
Sherlock Holmes, Halloween Fantasies
Sherlock Holmes, Halloween Terror
Sherlock Holmes, Halloween Terror 2

Watch for more at www.johnpirillo.com.